It's
Harlequin's 60th anniversary
this year!

**Harlequin Romance is going to shower you with…
diamond proposals and dazzling weddings,
sparkling brides and gorgeous grooms!**

The Australian's Society Bride
by Margaret Way

Her Valentine Blind Date
by Raye Morgan

The Royal Marriage Arrangement
by Rebecca Winters

Two Little Miracles
by Caroline Anderson

Manhattan Boss, Diamond Proposal
by Trish Wylie

The Bridesmaid and the Billionaire
by Shirley Jump

Whether it's the stunning solitaire ring
that he's offering, the beautiful white dress she's wearing
or the loving vows between them, these stories
will bring a touch of sparkle to your life….

Dear Reader,

It was a real pleasure to be asked by my editor to contribute to the DIAMOND BRIDES series in celebration of Harlequin's 60th anniversary. I had a few guidelines—a diamond, a marriage gone wrong and, oh, could we have twins?

Absolutely! It was a wonderful opportunity to let my imagination run riot, and it was great fun to write. Max was a very interesting man to get to know, and Julia was tough enough to stick to her guns and not back down on matters she felt were deeply important, so working through their issues with them while they learned the meaning of compromise was fascinating.

And the twins, of course, were a delight. I was thrilled to give them all back to each other, and give them their truly happy ending. I hope you enjoy reading it nearly as much as I enjoyed dreaming them up for you, and I give them to you with my love.

Best wishes and happy reading,

Caroline

CAROLINE ANDERSON

Two Little Miracles

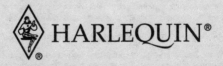

TORONTO • NEW YORK • LONDON
AMSTERDAM • PARIS • SYDNEY • HAMBURG
STOCKHOLM • ATHENS • TOKYO • MILAN • MADRID
PRAGUE • WARSAW • BUDAPEST • AUCKLAND

Recycling programs
for this product may
not exist in your area.

ISBN-13: 978-0-373-18424-8
ISBN-10:   0-373-18424-7

TWO LITTLE MIRACLES

First North American Publication 2009.

Copyright © 2008 by Caroline Anderson.

www.eHarlequin.com

Printed in U.S.A.

Caroline Anderson has the mind of a butterfly. She's been a nurse, a secretary, a teacher, has run her own soft-furnishing business and is now settled on writing. She says, "I was looking for that elusive something. I finally realized it was variety, and now I have it in abundance. Every book brings new horizons and new friends, and in between books I have learned to be a juggler. My teacher husband, John, and I have two beautiful and talented daughters, Sarah and Hannah, umpteen pets and several acres of Suffolk that nature tries to reclaim every time we turn our backs!" Caroline also writes for the Harlequin Medical™ Romance line.

Share your dream wedding proposal
and you could win a stunning diamond necklace!

For more information
visit www.DiamondBridesProposal.com.

PROLOGUE

'I'M NOT going with you.'

Her voice was unexpectedly loud in the quiet bedroom, and Max straightened up and stared at her.

'What? What do you mean, you're not coming with me? You've been working on this for weeks—what the hell can you possibly have found that needs doing before you can leave? And how long are you talking about? Tomorrow? Wednesday? I need you there now, Jules, we've got a lot to do.'

Julia shook her head. 'No. I mean, I'm not coming. Not going to Japan. Not today, not next week—not ever. Or anywhere else.'

She couldn't go.

Couldn't pack up her things and head off into the sunset—well, sunrise, to be tediously accurate, as they were flying to Japan.

Correction: *Max* was flying to Japan. She

wasn't. She wasn't going anywhere. Not again, not for the umpteenth time in their hectic, tempestuous, whirlwind life together. Been there, done that, et cetera. And she just couldn't do it any more.

He dropped the carefully folded shirt into his case and turned towards her, his expression incredulous. 'Are you serious? Have you gone crazy?'

'No. I've never been more serious about anything. I'm sick of it,' she told him quietly. 'I don't want to do it any more. I'm sick of you saying jump, and all I do is say, "How high?"'

'I never tell you to jump!'

'No. No, you're right. You tell me *you* need to jump, and I ask how high, and then I make it happen for you—in any language, in any country, wherever you've decided the next challenge lies.'

'You're my PA—that's your job!'

'No, Max. I'm your *wife*, and I'm sick of being treated like any other employee. And I'm not going to let you do it to me any more.'

He stared at her for another endless moment, then rammed his hands through his hair and glanced at his watch before reaching for another shirt. 'You've picked a hell of a time for a marital,' he growled, and, not for the first time, she wanted to scream.

'It's not a marital,' she said as calmly as she could manage. 'It's a fact. I'm not coming—and I don't know if I'll be here when you get back. I can't do it any more—any of it—and I need time to work out what I do want.'

His fists balled in the shirt, crushing it to oblivion, but she didn't care. It wasn't as if she'd been the one who'd ironed it. The laundry service took care of that. She didn't have time. She was too busy making sure the cogs were all set in motion in the correct sequence.

'Hell, Jules, your timing sucks.'

He threw the shirt into the case and stalked to the window, ramming his hand against the glass and staring out over the London skyline, his tall, muscled frame vibrating with tension. 'You know what this means to me—how important this deal is. Why today?'

'I don't know,' she said honestly. 'I just—I've hit a brick wall. I'm so sick of not having a life.'

'We have a life!' he roared, twisting away from the window and striding across to tower over her, his fists opening and closing in frustration. 'We have a damn good life.'

'No, we go to work.'

'And we're *stunningly* successful!'

'Business-wise, I agree—but it's not a life.'
She met his furious eyes head-on, refusing to
let him intimidate her. She was used to Max in
a temper, and he'd never once frightened her.
'Our home life isn't a success, because we don't
have a home life, Max. We didn't see your
family over Christmas, we've worked over New
Year—for God's sake, we watched the fire-
works out of the office window! And did you
know today's the last day for taking down the
decorations? We didn't even *have* any, Max.
We didn't *do* Christmas. It just happened all
around us while we carried on. And I want more
than that. I want—I don't know—a house, a
garden, time to potter amongst the plants, to
stick my fingers in the soil and smell the roses.'
Her voice softened. 'We never stop and smell
the roses, Max. Never.'

He frowned, let his breath out on a harsh
sigh, and stared at his watch. His voice when
he spoke was gruff.

'We have to go. We're going to miss our
flight. Take some time out, if that's what you
need, but come with me, Jules. Get a massage
or something, go and see a Zen garden, but for
God's sake stop this nonsense—'

'Nonsense?' Her voice was cracking, and she firmed it, but she couldn't get rid of the little shake in it. 'I don't believe you, Max. You haven't heard a damn thing I've said. I don't want to go to a Zen garden. I don't want a massage. I'm not coming. I need time—time to think, time to work out what I want from life— and I can't do that with you pacing around the hotel bedroom at four o'clock in the morning and infecting me with your relentless enthusiasm and hunger for power. I just can't do it, and I won't.'

He dashed his hand through his hair again, rumpling the dark strands and leaving them on end, and then threw his washbag in on top of the crumpled shirt, tossed in the shoes that were lying on the bed beside the case and slammed it shut.

'You're crazy. I don't know what's got into you—PMT or something. And anyway, you can't just walk out, you've got a contract.'

'A con—?' She laughed, a strange, high-pitched sound that fractured in the middle. 'So sue me,' she said bitterly, and, turning away, she walked out of their bedroom and into the huge open-plan living space with its spectacular view of the river before she did something she'd regret.

It was still dark, the lights twinkling on the water, and she stared at them until they blurred. Then she shut her eyes.

She heard the zip on his case as he closed it, the trundle of the wheels, the sharp click of his leather soles against the beautiful wooden floor.

'I'm going now. Are you coming?'

'No.'

'Are you sure? Because, if you don't, that's it. Don't expect me to run around after you begging.'

She nearly laughed at the thought, but her heart was too busy breaking. 'I don't.'

'Good. So long as we understand one another. Where's my passport?'

'On the table, with the tickets,' she said without turning round, and waited, her breath held.

Waited for what—some slight concession? An apology? No, never that. *I love you?* But she couldn't remember when he'd last said those words, and he didn't say them now. She heard his footsteps, the wheels of his case on the floor, the rattle of his keys, the rustle of paper as he picked up the flight details, his passport and tickets, then the click of the latch.

'Last call.'

'I'm not coming.'

'Fine. Suit yourself. You know where to find me when you change your mind.' Then there was a pause, and again she waited, but after an age he gave a harsh sigh and the door clicked shut.

Still she waited, till she heard the ping of the lift, the soft hiss of the door closing, the quiet hum as it sank down towards the ground floor.

Then she sat down abruptly on the edge of the sofa and jerked in a breath.

He'd gone. He'd gone, and he hadn't said a word to change her mind, not one reason why she should stay. Except that she'd be breaking her contract.

Her contract, of all things! All she wanted was some time to think about their lives, and, because she wouldn't go with him, he was throwing away their marriage and talking about a blasted *contract*!

'Damn you, Max!' she yelled, but her voice cracked and she started to cry, great, racking sobs that tore through her and brought bile to her throat.

She ran to the bathroom and was horribly, violently sick, then slumped trembling to the floor, her back propped against the wall, her legs huddled under her on the hard marble.

'I love you, Max,' she whispered. 'Why couldn't you listen to me? Why couldn't you give us a chance?'

Would she have gone with him if he'd stopped, changed his flight and told her he loved her—taken her in his arms and hugged her and said he was sorry?

No. And, anyway, that wasn't Max's style.

She could easily have cried again, but she wouldn't give him the satisfaction, so she pulled herself together, washed her face, cleaned her teeth and repaired her make-up. Then she went back out to the living room and picked up the phone.

'Jane?'

'Julia, hi, darling! How are you?'

'Awful. I've just left Max.'

'What! Where?'

'No—I've *left* him. Well, he's left me, really…'

There was a shocked silence, then Jane said something very rude under her breath. 'OK, where are you?'

'At the apartment. Janey, I don't know what to do—'

'Where's Max now?'

'On his way to Japan. I was supposed to be going, but I just couldn't.'

'Right. Stay there. I'm coming. Pack a case. You're coming to stay with me.'

'I'm packed,' she said.

'Not jeans and jumpers and boots, I'll bet. You've got an hour and a half. Sort yourself out and I'll be there. And find something warm; it's freezing up here.'

The phone went dead, and she went back into the bedroom and stared at her case lying there on the bed. She didn't even *own* any jeans these days. Or the sort of boots Jane was talking about.

Or did she?

She rummaged in the back of a wardrobe and found her old jeans, and a pair of walking boots so old she'd forgotten she still had them, and, pitching the sharp suits and the four-inch heels out of the case, she packed the jeans and boots, flung in her favourite jumpers and shut the lid.

Their wedding photo was on the dressing table, and she stared at it, remembering that even then they hadn't taken time for a honeymoon. Just a brief civil ceremony, and then their wedding night, when he'd pulled out all the stops and made love to her until neither of them could move.

She'd fallen asleep in his arms, as usual, but

unusually she'd woken in them, too, because for once he hadn't left the bed to start working on his laptop, driven by a restless energy that never seemed to wane.

How long ago it seemed.

She swallowed and turned away from the photo, dragged her case to the door and looked round. She didn't want anything else—any reminders of him, of their home, of their life.

She took her passport, though, not because she wanted to go anywhere but just because she didn't want Max to have it. It was a symbol of freedom, in some strange way, and besides she might need it for all sorts of things.

She couldn't imagine what, but it didn't matter. She tucked it into her handbag and put it with her case by the door, then she emptied the fridge into the bin and put it all down the rubbish chute and sat down to wait. But her mind kept churning, and so she turned on the television to distract her.

Not a good idea. Apparently, according to the reporter, today—the first Monday after New Year—was known as 'Divorce Monday', the day when, things having come to a head over Christmas and the New Year, thousands of women would contact a lawyer and start divorce proceedings.

Including her?

Two hours later she was sitting at Jane's kitchen table in Suffolk. She'd been fetched, tutted and clucked over, and driven straight here, and now Jane was making coffee.

And the smell was revolting.

'Sorry—I can't.'

And she ran for the loo and threw up again. When she straightened up, Jane was standing behind her, staring at her thoughtfully in the mirror. 'Are you OK?'

'I'll live. It's just emotion. I love him, Janey, and I've blown it, and he's gone, and I just hate it.'

Jane humphed, opened the cabinet above the basin and handed her a long box. 'Here.'

She stared at it and gave a slightly hysterical little laugh. 'A pregnancy test? Don't be crazy. You know I can't have children. I've got all that scarring from my burst appendix. I've had tests; there's no way. I can't conceive—'

'No such word as can't—I'm living proof. Just humour me.'

She walked out and shut the door, and with

a shrug Julia read the instructions. Pointless. Stupid. She couldn't be pregnant.

'What on earth am I going to do?'

'Do you want to stay with him?'

She didn't even have to think about it. Even as shocked and stunned as she was by the result, she knew the answer, and she shook her head. 'No. Max has always been really emphatic about how he didn't want children, and anyway, he'd have to change beyond recognition before I'd inflict him on a child. You know he told me I couldn't leave because I had a contract?'

Jane tsked softly. 'Maybe he was clutching at straws.'

'Max? Don't be ridiculous. He doesn't clutch at anything. Anyway, it's probably not an option. He told me, if I didn't go with him, that was it. But I have to live somewhere; I can't stay with you and Pete, especially as you're pregnant again, too. I think one baby's probably enough.' She gave a shaky laugh. 'I just can't *believe* I'm pregnant, after all these years.'

Jane laughed a little self-consciously. 'Well, it happens to the best of us. You're lucky I had the spare test. I nearly did another one because I didn't believe it the first time, but we've just about come to terms with it—and I'm even getting excited now about having another one, and the kids are thrilled. So,' she said, getting back to the point, 'Where do you want to live? Town or country?'

Julia tried to smile. 'Country?' she said tentatively. 'I really don't want to go back to London, and I know it's silly, and I've probably got incredibly brown thumbs, but I really want a garden.'

'A garden?' Jane tipped her head on one side, then grinned. 'Give me a minute.'

It took her five, during which time Julia heard her talking on the phone in the study next door, then she came back with a self-satisfied smile.

'Sorted. Pete's got a friend, John Blake, who's going to be working in Chicago for a year. He'd found someone to act as a caretaker for the house, but it's fallen through, and he's been desperately looking for someone else.'

'Why doesn't he just let it?'

'Because he'll be coming and going, so he can't really. But it's a super house, all your running and living expenses will be paid, all you have to do is live in it, not have any wild parties, and call the plumber if necessary. Oh, and feed and walk the dog. Are you OK with dogs?'

She nodded. 'I love dogs. I've always wanted one.'

'Brilliant. And Murph's a sweetie. You'll love him, and the house. It's called Rose Cottage, it's got an absolutely gorgeous garden, and the best thing is it's only three miles from here, so we can see lots of each other. It'll be fun.'

'But what about the baby? Won't he mind?'

'John? Nah. He loves babies. Anyway, he's hardly ever home. Come on, we're going to see him now.'

CHAPTER ONE

'I'VE found her.'

Max froze.

It was what he'd been waiting for since June, but now—now he was almost afraid to voice the question. His heart stalling, he leaned slowly back in his chair and scoured the investigator's face for clues. 'Where?' he asked, and his voice sounded rough and unused, like a rusty hinge.

'In Suffolk. She's living in a cottage.'

Living. His heart crashed back to life, and he sucked in a long, slow breath. All these months he'd feared…

'Is she well?'

'Yes, she's well.'

He had to force himself to ask the next question. 'Alone?'

The man paused. 'No. The cottage belongs to a man called John Blake. He's working away at the moment, but he comes and goes.'

God. He felt sick. So sick he hardly registered the next few words, but then gradually they sank in. 'She's got *what*?'

'Babies. Twin girls. They're eight months old.'

'Eight—?' he echoed under his breath. 'So he's got children?'

He was thinking out loud, but the PI heard and corrected him.

'Apparently not. I gather they're hers. She's been there since mid-January last year, and they were born during the summer—June, the woman in the post office thought. She was more than helpful. I think there's been a certain amount of speculation about their relationship.'

He'd just bet there had. God, he was going to kill her. Or Blake. Maybe both of them.

'Of course, looking at the dates, she was presumably pregnant when she left you, so they could be yours—or she could have been having an affair with this Blake character before.'

He glared at the unfortunate PI. 'Just stick to your job. I can do the maths,' he snapped, swallowing the unpalatable possibility that she'd been unfaithful to him before she'd left. 'Where is she? I want the address.'

'It's all in here,' the man said, sliding a

large envelope across the desk to him. 'With my invoice.'

'I'll get it seen to. Thank you.'

'If there's anything else you need, Mr Gallagher, any further information—'

'I'll be in touch.'

'The woman in the post office told me Blake was away at the moment, if that helps,' he added quietly, and opened the door.

Max stared down at the envelope, hardly daring to open it. But, when the door clicked softly shut behind the PI, he eased up the flap, tipped it and felt his breath jam in his throat as the photos spilled out over the desk.

Oh lord, she looked gorgeous. Different, though. It took him a moment to recognise her, because she'd grown her hair and it was tied back in a ponytail, making her look younger and somehow freer. The blonde highlights were gone, and it was back to its natural soft golden-brown, with a little curl in the end of the ponytail that he wanted to thread his finger through and tug, just gently, to draw her back to him.

Crazy. She'd put on a little weight, but it suited her. She looked well and happy and beautiful, but oddly, considering how desperate he'd been for news of her for the last year—one year, three weeks and two days, to be exact—it wasn't Julia who held his attention after the initial shock. It was the babies sitting side by side in a supermarket trolley. Two identical and absolutely beautiful little girls.

His? It was a distinct possibility. He only had to look at the dark, spiky hair on their little heads, so like his own at that age. He could have been looking at a photo of himself.

Max stared down at it until the images swam in front of his eyes. He pressed the heels of his hands against them, struggling for breath, then lowered his hands and stared again.

She was alive—alive and well—and she had two beautiful children.

Children that common sense would dictate were his.

Children he'd never seen, children he'd not been told about, and suddenly he found he couldn't breathe. Why hadn't she told him? Would he ever have been told about them? Damn it, how *dared* she keep them a secret from him? Unless they weren't his…

He felt anger building inside him, a terrible rage that filled his heart and made him want to destroy something the way she'd destroyed him.

The paperweight hit the window and shattered, the pieces bouncing off the glass and falling harmlessly to the floor, and he bowed his head and counted to ten.

'Max?'

'He's found her—in Suffolk. I have to go.'

'Of course you do,' his PA said soothingly. 'But take a minute, calm down, I'll make you a cup of tea and get someone to pack for you.'

'I've got a bag in the car. You'll have to cancel New York. In fact, cancel everything for the next two days. I'm sorry, Andrea, I don't want tea. I just want to see my—my wife.'

And the babies. His babies.

She blocked his path. 'It's been over a year, Max. Another ten minutes won't make any difference. You can't go tearing in there like this, you'll frighten the life out of her. You have to take it slowly, work out what you want to say. Now sit down. That's it. Did you have lunch?'

He sat obediently and stared at her, wondering what the hell she was talking about. 'Lunch?'

'I thought so. Tea and a sandwich—and then you can go.'

He stared after her—motherly, efficient, bossy, organising—and deeply, endlessly kind, he realised now—and felt his eyes prickle again.

He couldn't just sit there. He crunched over

the paperweight and placed his hands flat on the window, his forehead pressed to the cool, soothing glass. Why hadn't he known? How could she have kept something so significant from him for so long?

He heard the door open and Andrea return.

'Is this her?'

'Yes.'

'And the babies?'

He stared out of the window. 'Yes. Interesting, isn't it? It seems I'm a father, and she didn't even see fit to tell me. Either that or she's had an affair with my doppelganger, because they look just like I did.'

She put the tray down, tutted softly and then, utterly out of the blue, his elegant, calm, practical PA hugged him.

He didn't know what to do for a second. It was so long since anyone had held him that he was shocked at the contact. But then slowly he lifted his arms and hugged her back, and the warmth and comfort of it nearly unravelled him. Resisting the urge to hang on, he stepped back out of her arms and turned away, dragging in air and struggling for control of the situation.

'Goodness, aren't they like you?'

She was staring down at the photos on the desk, a smile on her face, and he nodded. 'Yes. Yes, they are. I've seen pictures of me—'

Was that his voice? He cleared his throat and tried again. 'I must have been that sort of age. My mother's got an album—' And then it hit him. She was a grandmother. He'd have to tell her. She'd be overjoyed.

Oh, hell. His eyes were at it again.

'Here, drink your tea and eat the sandwiches, and I'll get David to bring the car round.'

The car. A two-seater, low, sexy, gorgeous open-top sports car with a throaty growl and absolutely nowhere to put baby seats, he thought as he got into it a few minutes later. Never mind. He could change it. He tapped the address into the satnav and headed out of town, the hood down and the icy February wind in his hair, trying to blow away the cobwebs and help him think—because he still had no idea what on earth he was going to say to her.

He still had no idea nearly two hours later, when the satnav had guided him to the centre of the village, and he pulled up in the dusk and looked at the map the PI had given him.

There was the bridge over the river, just

ahead of him, so it should be here on the right, down this drive.

He dragged in a deep breath, shut the hood because he suddenly realised he was freezing and it was starting to mist with rain, and bumped slowly down the drive, coming out into an open area in front of the house.

He saw a pretty, thatched, chocolate-box cottage in the sweep of his headlights, and then he saw her walking towards the window in a room to the right of the front door, a baby in her arms, and his heart jammed in his throat.

'Shush, Ava, there's a good girl. Don't cry, darling— Oh, look, there's somebody coming! Shall we see who it is? It might be Auntie Jane!'

She went to the window and looked out as the headlights sliced across the gloom and the car came to rest, and felt the blood drain from her face.

Max! How—?

She sat down abruptly on the old sofa in the bay window, ignoring the baby chewing her fist and grizzling on her shoulder, and her sister joining in from the playpen. Because all she could do was stare at Max getting out of the car, unfurling his long body, slamming the door, walking slowly and purposefully towards the porch.

The outside lights had come on, but he must be able to see her in the kitchen with the lights on, surely? Any second now.

He clanged the big bell and turned away, his shoulders rigid with tension, hands jammed into the pockets of his trousers, pushing the jacket out of the way and ruining the beautiful cut.

He was thinner, she realised—because of course without her there to nag and organise he wouldn't be looking after himself—and she felt a flicker of guilt and promptly buried it.

This was all his fault. If he'd listened to her, paid more attention last year when she'd said she wasn't happy, actually stopped and discussed it— But no.

Don't expect me to run around after you begging. You know where to find me when you change your mind.

But she hadn't, and of course he hadn't contacted her. She'd known he wouldn't—Max didn't beg—and she'd just let it drift, not knowing what to do once she'd realised she was pregnant, just knowing she couldn't go back to that same situation, to that same man.

Even if she still cried herself to sleep at night

because she missed him. Even if, every time she looked at his children, she felt a huge well of sadness that they didn't know the man who was their father. But how to tell him, when he'd always said so emphatically that it was the last thing he wanted?

Then Murphy whined, ran back to the door and barked, and Ava gave up grizzling and let out a full-blown yell, and he turned towards the window and met her eyes.

She was so close.

Just there, on the other side of the glass, one of the babies in her arms, and there was a dog barking, and he didn't know what to do.

You can't go tearing in there like this, you'll frighten the life out of her. You have to take it slowly, work out what you want to say. Oh Andrea, so sage, so sensible. Jules would approve of you.

But he still didn't know what on earth he was going to say to her.

He ought to smile, he thought, but his mouth wasn't working, and he couldn't drag his eyes from her face. She looked—hell, she looked exhausted, really, but he'd never seen anything more beautiful or welcome in his life. Then she turned away, and he felt his hand reach out to the glass as if to stop her.

But she was only coming to the door, he realised a second later, and he sagged against the wall with a surge of relief. A key rattled, and the big oak door swung in, and there she was, looking tired and pale, but more beautiful than he'd ever seen her, with the baby on her hip and a big black Labrador at her side.

'Hello, Max.'

That was it? A year, two children, a secret relationship and all she could say was *'Hello, Max'*?

He didn't know what he'd expected, but it wasn't that. He felt bile rise in his throat, driven by a rage so all-consuming it was threatening to destroy him from the inside out—a year of grief and fear and anger all coming to a head in that moment—but he remembered Andrea's words and tamped it down hard. He could do this, he told himself, so he gritted his teeth and met her eyes.

'Hello, Julia.'

He was propped against the wall, one arm up at shoulder height, his hair tousled and wind-swept, his eyes dark and unreadable. Only the jumping muscle in his jaw gave him away, and she realised he knew.

'Hello, Julia.'

Julia, not Jules. That was a change. She wondered what else had changed. Not enough, probably. Inevitably. She gathered her composure and straightened up, taking control of the situation if not her trembling body.

'You'd better come in,' she said. After all, what else could she do? She had a feeling he was coming in if he had to break the door down, so she might as well do this the easy way.

He followed her back to the kitchen, his footsteps loud on the tiles, and she could hear Murphy fussing around him and thrashing his tail into all the furniture and doors. She thought of Max's suit and how it would look decorated in dog hair, and stifled a smile. He'd hate that. He was always so particular.

'Shut the door, keep the heat in,' she instructed, and he shut it and turned towards her, that muscle jumping in his jaw again.

'Is that all you've got to say? A whole year without a word, and all you've got to say is "Shut the door"?'

'I'm trying to keep the babies warm,' she said, and his eyes tracked immediately to the baby in her arms, his expression unreadable. Supremely conscious of the monumental nature of the moment, she locked her legs to stop them shaking and said, 'This is Ava,' and, gesturing with her free hand towards the lobster-pot playpen near the Aga, added, 'and this is Libby.'

And, hearing her name, Libby looked up, took the bubbly, spitty teething ring out of her mouth and grinned. 'Mum-mum,' she said, and, holding up her arms, she opened and closed her hands, begging to be picked up.

Julia went to move towards her, then stopped and looked at Max, her heart pounding. 'Well, go on, then. Pick up your daughter. I take it that's why you're here?'

He was transfixed.

Your daughter.

Oh lord. It was ages since he'd held a baby. He wasn't even sure he'd ever held one this age. Older, yes, and probably walking, but not small, dribbly and gummy and quite so damned appealing, and he was suddenly terrified he'd drop her.

He shrugged off his jacket and hung it over a chair, then reached into the playpen, put his hands under her armpits and lifted her out.

'She's light! I thought she'd be heavier.'

'She's only a baby, Max, and twins are often

small, but don't be scared of her. They're remarkably robust. Say hello to Daddy, Libby.'

Daddy?

'Mum-mum,' she said, and, reaching up, she grabbed his nose and pulled it hard.

'Ouch.'

'Libby, gently,' Julia said, easing her fingers away, and told him to put her on his hip, then handed him Ava, settling her in the curve of his other arm. 'There you go. Your children.'

He stared down at them. They were like peas in a pod, he thought, wondering how on earth she told them apart, and they smelt extraordinary. Like nothing he'd ever smelt before. Sweet and clean, and somehow…

Then Ava reached out to Libby, and they beamed at each other and turned and stared up at him with brilliant blue eyes exactly the colour of his own, and they smiled at him in unison, and, without warning, Max fell headlong in love.

'Here, you'd better sit down,' Julia said with a lump in her throat, and pulled a chair out from the table and steered him towards it before his legs gave way. He had a thunder-struck look on his face, and the girls were clearly as fascinated as he was. They were pawing his face, pulling his ears, grabbing his nose and twisting it, and he just sat there looking amazed and let them do it.

Then he looked up at her, and she saw that behind the burgeoning love in his eyes was a simmering anger fiercer than any she'd ever seen before, and she fell back a step.

He hated her.

She could see it in his eyes, in the black, bitter rage that filled them, and she turned away, tears welling. 'I'll put the kettle on,' she said, more to give her something to do than anything. But then Ava started to cry again, and Libby whimpered, and she plonked the kettle down on the hob and turned back and took Ava from him.

'Come on, sweetheart,' she murmured, her voice sounding fractured and uncertain, and Ava picked up on it and threw herself backwards. She caught her easily, snuggling her close, and the baby started to tug at her jumper.

Oh, hell. Her breasts were prickling, the babies needed feeding, and Max—Max, who knew her body better than she knew it herself— was sitting there watching her with black, brooding eyes.

'I need to feed her,' she said, and then Libby joined in and started to yell. 'Both of them.'

'I'll help you.'

'I don't think you can. You don't have the equipment,' she said with an attempt at levity, and as the penny dropped a dull flush of colour ran over his cheekbones.

'Um—here,' he said, handing Libby to her. 'I'll—um—'

'Oh, sit down, Max,' she said, giving up and heading for the sofa in the bay window. There was no point in procrastinating. And, anyway, he wasn't going to see anything he hadn't seen before. She sat down, pulled the cushions round to rest the babies on, one each side, undid her bra, pushed it out of the way and plugged them in.

He didn't know where to look.

He knew where he wanted to look. Couldn't drag his eyes away, in fact, but he didn't think it was exactly polite to stare.

He stifled a cough of laughter. Polite? This situation was so far from being *polite* that it was positively off the chart, but he still couldn't sit there and stare.

'Kettle's boiling. I'd love a cup of tea,' she said, and he realised she was looking at him.

'Ah—sure.'

He got up, went over to the Aga and lifted the kettle off, then didn't know where to put it. On the lid? Maybe. He put the lid down, then realised there was room beside it. What a ridiculous system. What on earth was wrong with an electric kettle or the tap for boiling water they had in their apartment?

Their apartment?

Still? A year later?

'Where are the mugs?'

'Over the sink. The tea's in the caddy there by the Aga, and the milk's in the fridge in the utility room. Put some cold water in mine, please.'

He put the teabags in the mugs, stepped over the dog, fetched the milk and sloshed it in the tea, then put the milk away, stepping over the dog again, and took Julia her mug.

'Thanks. Just put it there on the end of the table,' she said, and he set it down and hesitated.

He could see the babies' mouths working on Julia's nipples, a bluish film of milk around their lips, fat little hands splayed out over the swollen white orbs of her breasts. They were so much bigger than normal, the skin on them laced faintly with blue veins, and he was fascinated. There was just something basic and fundamental and absolutely *right* about it.

And he felt excluded.

Isolated and cut off, kept out of this precious

and amazing event which had taken place without him.

Cheated.

He turned away, taking his tea and propping himself morosely against the front of the Aga, huddling against its warmth. He felt cold right to his bones, chilled by his exclusion. And angry.

So furiously bloody angry that he was ready to hit something. A door? A wall? Not Jules. Never Jules, no matter how much she might infuriate him. It was only his surroundings that bore the brunt of his recent ill-temper, and right then he was ready to tear the house apart.

'Max?'

He glanced across at her.

'Could you take Ava for me? She's finished, she just needs to burp. Could you walk round with her? Oh, and you'd better have this; she might bring up some milk on you.'

She handed him a soft white cloth—a muslin nappy; how did he know that?—and then his daughter. His precious, precious daughter. God, that was going to take some getting used to. She was sunny now, all smiles again, but then she burped and giggled, and he wiped her mouth with the corner of the cloth and smiled at her.

'Lager lout,' he said with an unaccustomed

wave of affection, and she giggled again and grabbed his nose. 'Hey, gently,' he murmured, removing her hand, and, lifting his tea to his mouth, he was about to take a sip when her hand flew up and caught the mug and sent it all over him.

Without thinking he swung her out of the way, but there was nothing he could do to save himself from it and it was hot—hot enough to make him yelp with shock—and Ava screwed up her face and screamed. Oh, lord. Water. Cold water. He carried her to the tap and sloshed cold water over her, holding her hand under the dribbling tap just in case, while Julia put Libby down and ran over.

'Give her to me,' she said, and quickly laid her on the table and stripped off her clothes. The muslin nappy had caught most of it, and there wasn't a mark on her, but it could so easily have been a disaster, and he felt sick. Sick and stupid and irresponsible.

'What the hell did you think you were doing? You don't hold a cup of boiling tea over a child!' Julia raged, and he stepped back, devastated that he might so easily have caused his tiny daughter harm.

'I'm sorry. I didn't think— Is she all right? Does she need to go to hospital?'

'No, you must have missed her, she's fine—no thanks to you.'

'You gave her to me.'

'I didn't expect you to pour tea over her!'

'It missed her.'

'Only by the grace of God! It could have gone all over her! Of all the stupid, stupid—'

'You were holding your tea over them!'

'It had cold water in it! What do you think that was for? Shush, sweetheart, it's OK.' But the babies were both screaming now, upset by the shouting and the whining of the dog, and he stepped back again, shaking his head.

'I'm sorry,' he said roughly. 'Jules, I'm so sorry—'

He scrubbed his hand through his hair and turned away, furious with himself for his stupidity, but he wasn't to be allowed to wallow.

'Here, hold her. I need to change her. I'll get her some clean, dry clothes.' And then she paused and looked up at him, her lashes spiked with tears, and her voice softened. 'She's all right, Max. It was just the shock. I'm sorry I yelled at you.'

'She could have been—' He broke off, and Julia's face contorted.

'Don't. It was an accident. Just hold her. I'll only be a moment.'

He didn't move a muscle. Just stood there, motionless, until she came back into the room armed with nappies and tiny clothes, and took the screaming baby out of his arms. Then he sat down, buried his face in his hands and sucked in a breath.

'Can you cuddle Libby, please?'

He pulled himself together and sat up. 'Do you trust me?' he asked tersely, and she gave him a grim smile.

'I have to, don't I? You're their father.'

'Am I?'

'Max, of course you are! Who else?'

'I don't know, but perhaps we should get a DNA test.'

Her face went white. 'Whatever for? I wouldn't lie to you about that. And I'm not about to start asking you for money to support us, either.'

'I wasn't thinking about money, I was thinking about paternity. And I wouldn't have thought you would lie about it, but then I wouldn't have thought you'd leave me without warning, shack up with another man and have two children without bothering to share the information with me. So clearly I don't know you nearly as well as I thought I did and, yes, I want a DNA test,' he said, his anger rising to the surface again. 'Because, apart from anything else, it might be handy in court.'

'Court?' She looked aghast. 'Why court? I'm not going to do anything to obstruct your access.'

'I don't know that. You might move again— go into hiding somewhere else. I know you've got your passport with you. But on the other hand, if you decide to go for maintenance, I want to be damn sure it's *my* kids I'm paying for.'

She gasped, her eyes wounded, and he felt a total heel.

'Don't bother to turn the tears on,' he growled, hating it—because he thought she was going to cry and Jules never, ever cried—but his words rallied her and she straightened up and glared at him.

'I'd forgotten what a bastard you are, Max. You don't need a test to prove you're the father! You were with me every minute of the day and night when they were conceived. Who else could it possibly have been?'

He shrugged. 'John Blake?'

She stared at him, then started to laugh. 'John? No. No, John's not a threat to you. Trust me. Apart from the fact that he's in his late fifties and definitely not my type, he's gay.'

The surge of relief was so great it took his breath away. She hadn't had an affair—and the babies were his. Definitely.

And one of them was still screaming for attention.

He picked Libby up, moving almost on autopilot, and went over to where Julia was dressing Ava. She ran her eyes over his chest. 'Your shirt's soaked. Are you all right?' she asked, without a flicker of compassion, and he told himself he didn't deserve it anyway.

'I'm sure I'll live,' he replied tersely. 'Is she really OK?'

'She's fine, Max,' Julia said, her voice grudging but fair as ever. 'It was an accident. Don't worry about it.'

Easy to say, not so easy to do. Especially when, some time later, after they'd been fed little pots of disgusting-smelling goo—how lamb and vegetables could possibly smell so vile he had no idea—Julia put the babies down in their cots for a sleep and made him take off his shirt, and he saw the reddened skin over his chest and shoulder. If that had been Ava…

He nearly retched with the thought, but Julia's soft sound of dismay stopped him in his tracks.

'Idiot. You told me you were all right!' she

scolded softly, guilt in her eyes, and then spread something green and cool over his skin with infinite gentleness.

'What's that?' he asked, his voice a little hoarse, because it was so long since she'd touched him that the feel of her fingers on his skin was enough to take the legs out from under him.

'It's aloe vera gel,' she murmured. 'It's good for burns.'

And then she looked up and met his eyes, and time stopped. He couldn't breathe, his heart was lodged in his throat, and for the life of him he couldn't look away.

He wanted her.

He was still furious with her for keeping the babies from him, for leaving him without warning and dropping off the face of the earth, but he'd never stopped loving her, and he loved her now.

'Jules—'

She stepped back, the spell broken by the whispered word, and screwed the lid back on the gel, but her fingers were trembling, and for some crazy reason that gave him hope.

'You need a clean shirt. Have you got anything with you?'

'Yes, in the car. I've got a case with me.'

She looked back at him, her eyes widening.

'You're planning on staying?' she said in a breath-less whisper, and he gave a short huff of laughter.

'Oh yes. Yes, Jules, I'm staying, because, now I've found you, I'm not losing sight of you or my children again.'

CHAPTER TWO

HE WENT out to his car to get a dry shirt, and she watched him through the window, her hand over her mouth.

He was staying?

Oh, lord. Staying *here*? No! No, he couldn't stay here, not with her! She couldn't let him get that close, because she knew him, knew that look in his eyes, knew just how vulnerable she was to his potent sexual charm. He'd only have to touch her and she'd crumple like a wet tissue.

She was shocked at the change in him, though.

He'd lost weight; she'd been right. He was thinner, the taut muscles right there under her fingers as she'd smoothed the gel on his reddened skin. His hair was touched with grey at the temples, and he looked every one of his thirty-eight years. He'd aged in the last year more than he'd aged in all the years she'd known him, and she felt another stab of guilt.

She told herself it wasn't her fault he didn't look after himself, but she hadn't expected him to look so—so *ravaged*. His ribs had been clearly visible in the kitchen light, but so, too, had every muscle and sinew, and she realised that, although he was thinner and looked driven, he was fit.

Fit and lean and hard, and she felt her mouth dry as he got his case out of the boot, plipped the remote control and headed back towards the door, showing her the firm definition of those muscles and ribs in the harsh security lighting. He'd been working out, she thought. Or running. Or both. He often did, usually when things were tricky and he needed to think.

Or to stop himself thinking.

Was that her fault? Possibly. Probably. Oh hell, it was such a mess, and just to make things worse he'd scalded himself when Ava had lunged at him. He must be freezing, she thought, with that wet gel over his burn. It wasn't bad really, but he'd looked so stricken when he'd seen the pink mark across his skin, as if he'd been thinking that it could have been Ava, and she felt dreadful for shouting at him.

She'd just been so tense, and it had been the last straw.

'Is there a pub or somewhere I can stay?' he

asked, coming back into the kitchen and crouching down to open his case, pulling out a soft sweater and dragging it over his head in place of the shirt.

She opened her mouth to say yes, but some demon in his pay had control of it, because all that came out was, 'Don't be silly, you can stay here. There are plenty of rooms.'

'Really?' he asked, studying her with concern, and something else that might have been mockery in his eyes. 'Aren't you worried that I'll compromise your position in the village?'

She laughed at that. 'It's a bit late to worry about compromising me, Max,' she said softly. 'You did that when you got me pregnant. And frankly the village can take a running jump.'

He frowned, and turned his attention back to his case, zipping it shut and standing it in the corner. 'What about Blake?' he asked, his mouth taut.

'What about him? I'm caretaking. I'm allowed visitors, it's in my agreement.'

'You have an agreement?'

'Well, of course I have an agreement!' she said. 'What did you think, I was just shacked up with some random man? He's a friend of

Jane and Peter's, and he was looking for someone to house-sit. Don't worry, it's all above board.'

'The woman in the post office seemed to think otherwise.'

'The woman in the post office needs to get a life,' she said briskly. 'Anyway, as I've already told you, he's gay. Are you hungry?'

He frowned. 'Hungry?'

'Max, you need to eat,' she said, feeling another stab of guilt over who if anyone fed him these days, who told him when he'd worked late enough and that it was too early to get up, who stopped him burning the candle at both ends and in the middle.

Nobody, she realised in dismay, looking at him really closely. Nobody at all, and least of all himself. He was exhausted, dark hollows round his eyes, his mouth drawn, that lovely ready smile gone without trace.

She felt tears filling her eyes, and turned away.

'There's some chicken in the fridge, or I've got all sorts of things in the freezer.'

'Can't we go out?'

'Where, with the twins?'

His face was a picture, and she shook her head and stifled a laugh. 'I can't just go out,

Max. It's a military operation, and I don't have instant access to a babysitter.'

'Does the pub do food?'

'Yes. It's good, too. You could go over there.'

'Would they deliver?'

'I doubt it.'

'I could offer them an incentive.'

'I'm sure you could,' she said drily. 'Why don't you go down there and sweet-talk them? It's only just the other side of the river. It'll take you two minutes to walk it. Or you could just eat there if you're worried I'll poison you.'

He ignored that. 'Do they have a menu?'

'They do. They're very good. It's a sort of gastro-pub. You could choose something and have a drink while they cook it. It'll take about twenty minutes, probably.'

And she could have a shower and change into something that didn't smell of baby sick and nappy cream, and brush her hair and put on some make-up— No, no make-up, she didn't want to look too desperate, but she could call Jane.

'It's a bit early. I could go later.'

'Except the babies may wake later, and it's easier to eat when they're asleep. Besides, they only serve until nine, and anyway I'm starving. I forgot about lunch.'

Still he hesitated, but then he gave a curt nod, shrugged on his jacket and headed for the door. 'What do you fancy?'

'Anything. You know what I like.'

He sipped his beer morosely and stared at the menu.

Did he know what she liked? He used to think so. Skinny sugar-free vanilla lattes, bacon rolls, almond croissants, really bitter dark chocolate, steamed vegetables, pan-fried sea bass, a well-chilled Chablis, sticky-toffee pudding with thick double cream—and waking up on Sunday morning at home in their apartment and making love until lunchtime.

He'd known how to wring every last sigh and whimper out of her, how to make her beg and plead for more, for that one last touch, the final stroke that would drive her screaming over the edge.

'Are you ready to order, sir?'

He closed his eyes briefly and then looked up at the pretty young waitress with what he hoped was something resembling a normal smile. 'Um—yes. I'll have the rib-eye steak, please—rare—and the—' He hesitated. The pan-fried salmon, or the chicken breast stuffed with brie and pesto?

Then he remembered her saying she had chicken in the fridge. 'I'll have the salmon, please. And I'd like to take them away, if you can do that for me? I know you don't usually, but we don't have a babysitter and, well, it's the closest we can get to going out for dinner. I'll drop the plates back tomorrow.' This time the smile was better, less jerky and awkward, and she coloured slightly and smiled back.

'I'm sure we can do that for you, sir,' she said a little breathlessly, and he hated himself for the little kick of pride that he could still make the girls go silly with a simple smile.

'Oh, and could I have a look at the wine list? I'd like to take a couple of bottles home, if I may?'

'Of course, sir. I'll take this to the kitchen and bring the wine list back to you.'

She was back with it in moments, and he chose a red and a white, paid the bill and settled back to wait.

Funny. This time yesterday he would have been too busy to wait for his food. He would have had it delivered. Even if they didn't deliver, he would have had it delivered, because everything had a price. You just had to pay enough.

But tonight, after he'd made a couple of phone calls and checked his email on his Black-Berry® Smartphone, he was glad just to sit there in the busy pub, which was more of a restaurant than a watering hole, and take time out from what had been probably the most momentous day of his life. Unless…

But he didn't want to think about that other day, so he buried the thought and tapped his fingers and waited…

'That was lovely. Thank you, Max. It was a really nice idea.'

'Was it all right? My steak was good, but I knew you wouldn't want that, and I thought the fish was safe, but I didn't know if you'd want a pudding.' He frowned. 'I realised I didn't know what you would want.'

She felt the smile coming and couldn't stop it. 'You aren't alone. I often don't know what I want.'

One brow flew up in frank disbelief. 'Are you telling me you've become indecisive?'

She laughed at that. 'I've always been indecisive if it affects me personally. I've just trained myself to remember that I'm going to eat it, not marry it, so it really doesn't matter that much. Well, not with food, anyway. Other things—well, they're harder,' she admitted slowly.

His eyes turned brooding as he studied her. 'Is that why you didn't contact me? Because you couldn't decide if it was the right thing to do?'

She looked down, guilt and remorse flooding her. 'Probably. But you just wouldn't listen, so there didn't seem to be any point in trying to talk to you—and you hadn't tried to talk to me, either.'

He sighed shortly. 'Because I told you to get in touch when you wanted me.' He paused, then added, 'The fact that you didn't…'

She nearly let that go, but in the end she couldn't. There was just something in his eyes she couldn't ignore. 'I nearly did. So many times. But I told myself that if you were prepared to listen, to talk about it, you'd ring me. And you didn't.'

'I tried. I couldn't get you. Your number was blocked and I had no idea why.'

'My phone was stolen. But that wasn't till June! So you didn't try for nearly six months, at least.'

He looked away, his jaw working, so she knew before he spoke that she was right. 'I was waiting for you to call me. I thought, if I gave you space—and when you didn't call a bit of me thought, to hell with you, really. But then I couldn't stand it any longer—the uncertainty. Not knowing where you were, what you were doing. It was killing me. So I called, and then I couldn't get you. And you weren't spending any money, you weren't using your account.'

'John pays my living expenses and runs the car.'

'Very generous,' he growled.

'He is. He's a nice man.'

His jaw clenched at that—at the thought of another man supporting her. Well, tough. He'd get over it. It was only a job.

'He's been marvellous,' she went on, turning the screw a little further. 'He was really understanding when the babies were born, and he got a friend to stay until I was able to come home.'

'Home?'

She smiled at him wryly. 'Yes, home. This is home for us—for now, anyway.' She didn't tell him that John was returning soon and she'd have to find somewhere else. Let him think everything was all right and there was no pressure on her, or he'd use it to push her into some kind of reconciliation, and she wasn't buying that until she was sure he was ready for it. If ever.

'That's when my phone was stolen, in the hospital, and I reported it and had the card blocked. But Jane gave me her old pay-as-you-go to use for emergencies, so I cancelled the contract. There didn't seem to be any point in paying an expensive tariff when most of the time I'm at home with the babies and I've got the landline.'

'And you didn't think to give me either of those numbers?'

She laughed a little bitterly. 'What, because you'd phoned me so regularly over the previous six months?'

His jaw clenched. 'It wasn't that. I told myself you'd contact me if you wanted me. I made myself give you space, give you time to sort out what you wanted. You said you needed time to think, but then I wondered how much time it could possibly take. If you needed that much, then we probably didn't have anything worth saving in your eyes, and I was damned if I was going to weaken and call you. But then when I couldn't get hold of you I got a PI on the job—'

'A PI!' she exclaimed, her guilt and sympathy brushed aside in an instant as her anger resurrected itself. 'You've had someone spying on me?'

'Because I was worried sick about you! And,

anyway, how the hell do you think I found you? Not by accident, all the way out here.'

'Well, not by trawling round yourself, that's for sure,' she said drily, ignoring yet another twinge of guilt. 'You'd be too busy to do that kind of thing yourself. I'm surprised you're here now, actually. Shouldn't you be somewhere more important?'

He gave her a sharp look. 'If it was more important, I'd *be* in New York now,' he growled, and she shook her head, the guilt retreating.

'I might have known. So when did you find out I was here?'

'Today. This afternoon—two-thirty or so.'

'Today?' she said, astonished. She'd thought, when he said about the PI, that he'd known where she was for ages. 'So you came straight here?'

He shrugged. 'What was I supposed to do? Wait for you to disappear again? Of course I came straight here—because I wanted answers.'

'You haven't asked me any questions yet— apart from why didn't I contact you, which I've told you.'

'And who's the father.'

She sat up straighter and glared at him. 'You *knew* they were yours! You weren't the slightest bit surprised. I expect your private eye took photos!'

He held her furious glare, but there was a

flicker of something that might—just might—have been guilt. She ignored it and ploughed on.

'Anyway, why would you care? You told me so many times you didn't want children. So what's changed, Max? What's brought you all the way up to sleepy old Suffolk in the depths of winter to ask me that?'

He was still looking her straight in the eye, but for the first time she felt she could really see past the mask, and her traitorous heart softened at the pain she saw there. 'You have,' he said gruffly. 'I've missed you, Jules. Come back to me.'

Oh no, Jane had been right, he was going to do the sweet-talking thing, but she'd been warned, and she wasn't falling for it. 'It's not that easy.'

'Oh, you're going to start the lifestyle thing again, aren't you?' he said, rolling his eyes and letting out his breath on a huff.

'Well—yes. You obviously haven't changed; you look dreadful, Max. How much sleep did you have last night?'

'Four hours,' he admitted grudgingly, looking a little uncomfortable.

'Four hours of sleep, or four hours in the apartment?'

'Sleep,' he said, but he looked uncomfortable

again, and she had a feeling he was hiding something, and she had a feeling she knew what.

'Max, how many hours are you working at the moment, on average? Fifteen? Eighteen? Twenty?' she added, watching him carefully, and she saw the slight movement when she hit the nail on the head. 'Max, you idiot, you can't do that! You need more than four hours' sleep! And where *are* you sleeping? The apartment, or in the office?'

'Why do you care?' he asked, his voice suddenly bitter, and he lifted his head and seared her with his eyes. 'What the hell is it to you if I burn myself out trying to—?'

'Trying to?' she coaxed, but then wished she hadn't because, his voice raw, he answered her with an honesty that flayed her heart.

'Trying to forget you. Trying to stay awake long enough that I fall asleep through sheer exhaustion and don't just lie there wondering if you're alive or dead.'

She sucked in her breath. 'Max—why would you think I was dead?'

'Because I heard nothing from you!' he grated, thrusting himself up out of the chair and prowling round the kitchen, the suppressed emotion making his body vibrate almost visibly. 'What was I supposed to think, Julia? That you were OK and everything was fine in La-La Land? Don't be so bloody naïve. You weren't spending anything, your phone wasn't working—you could have been lying in a ditch! I've spent the days searching for you, phoning everyone I could think of, nagging the backside off the PI, getting through PAs like a hot knife through butter, working myself to a standstill so I could fall over at the end of the day so tired I didn't have the energy or emotion left to—'

He broke off and turned away, spinning on his heel and slamming his hand against the wall while she stared at him, aghast at the pain in his words—pain that she'd caused.

Didn't have the energy or emotion left to— what? Cry himself to sleep, as she did?

No. Not Max.

Surely not?

She got up and crossed over to him, her socks silent on the stone-flagged floor, and laid a hand on his shoulder. 'Max, I'm so sorry,' she whispered, and he turned and dropped his shoulders against the wall and stared down at her.

'Why, Jules?' he asked, his voice like gravel. 'Why? What did I ever do to you that was so bad that you could treat me like that? How could you not have told me that I was going to be a father?'

'I wanted to, but you were always so anti-children—'

'Because you couldn't have any, and because—'

'Because?'

He shook his head. 'It doesn't matter. It's irrelevant now, but we were talking theory, there, not practice. When you found out you were pregnant— When did you find out, by the way?'

She swallowed. 'While you were on your way to Tokyo. Jane took one look at me and gave me her spare pregnancy test.'

His eyes widened. 'All that time? Right from the very first minute you knew, and you kept it from me? Jules—how? Why?'

'I didn't think you'd want to know. I wanted to tell you—I wanted so much for you to be there with me, to share it.'

'I would have been,' he said gruffly, his eyes tormented. 'I would have been with you every step of the way if you'd given me the chance.'

'But only when you weren't too busy.'

He looked away. 'I wouldn't have been too busy for that.'

'Of course you would.'

'No. Not for something like that. You should have given me the choice, Julia, not taken that decision away from me. You had no right to do that.'

He was right, of course. So right, and his anger and grief at the lost time cut right through her. She wanted to hold him, to put her arms round him, but she had no right to do that any more. How could she comfort him for the hurt she'd caused? And anyway there was no guarantee he wouldn't reject her, and she couldn't stand that.

And then he looked up and met her eyes, and she realised he wouldn't reject her at all. She was locked in the blue fire of his gaze, unable to breath for the emotion flooding through her.

He reached out his hand and cupped her cheek tenderly, and she realised his fingers were trembling. 'I need you,' he said under his breath. 'I hate you for what you've done to me, but, God damn you, I still need you. Come back to me. Please—come back to me; let's make a life together. We can start again.'

She stepped back, her legs like jelly. It would be so easy...

'I can't. Not to that life.'

'To what, then?'

She shrugged. 'I don't know. Just not that. Not the endless jetting round the world, the profit-chasing and the thrill of the stock market, the crazy takeovers, the race to the top of the rich list—I don't want to know any more, Max, and I can't do it, especially not with the babies. That's why I left you, and nothing's changed, has it? You should be in New York now, and, OK, you're here—but I bet you've been on the phone while you were in the pub or on the way over, or on the drive up here, or later after I go to bed you'll find calls you have to make. Am I right?' she pushed, and he sighed and nodded.

'Yes, damn it, you're right, of course you're right, but I have a business to run.'

'And staff. Good staff. Some excellent people, who are more than capable of keeping things going. So let them, Max. Give them a chance to prove themselves, and take time out to get to know your children.'

'Time?' he asked cautiously, as if it was a foreign concept, and she would have smiled if her life hadn't depended on it. As it was she was on the verge of tears, and she tilted her chin and put a little backbone into her voice.

'Two weeks. Two weeks here, with me, with no phones, no news, no papers, no laptop or email or post—just us. A holiday—you know, one of those things we've never had? You, me and the babies, to see if there's any way we can make a family.'

He was shaking his head. 'I can't take two weeks—not just like that. Not without any contact.'

'You can contact them and tell them,' she said. 'I know you'll need to do that. Look, I can't talk about this any more. It's been a hell of a day, and I'm shattered. I'm going to bed, and I suggest you do, too. You can have the room beyond the babies, it's all ready. And think about what I said. If you're really serious about us getting back together, then I want that two weeks. No compromises, no cheating, no bending the rules. Just you, me and the babies. Phone your PA and fix it first thing in the morning.'

One of those elegant, autocratic brows gave an ironic quirk. 'That sounds very much like an order.'

'Just laying down the ground rules. Either you're going to engage with this or you're not.'

'Just give me one good reason why I should.'

She laughed softly. 'I can give you two— and if you want to be part of their lives you'll do this. Because I'm not subjecting them to an absentee father who can't keep his family commitments and doesn't know the difference between work and home.'

He stared at her searchingly for the longest moment, then, just when she thought he'd refuse, he nodded.

'OK. I'll call Andrea in the morning and set it up. And you can have your two weeks. But make no mistake, I'm doing this for the children, because you're right—they deserve more than an absentee father. But it's going to take a long while before I can forgive you for cheating me of their first months, and for keeping something so monumentally important from me. So don't expect me to be all sweetness and light, because I'm still so angry with you I can't even find the words for it.'

Her eyes filled, and she swallowed the tears. 'I know. And I'm sorry. I didn't mean to hurt you, but, for what it's worth, I still love you.'

'You still love me? You can stand there and say that, and yet you walked out and didn't come back?' he said incredulously.

'Because it was killing me,' she told him unevenly. 'And I couldn't remember who we were. But I do still love you. That's never been in doubt.'

'Then come back to me.'

'No. Not just like that. It's not enough, not on its own. There has to be more. And I want to know if we've got anything left, when our old life's stripped away and all we've got to fall back on is each other. I think we could both be in for a shock.'

CHAPTER THREE

'ANDREA, it's—'

'Max! Are you all right?'

He blinked, a little startled by her concern. 'Fine,' he lied. 'I'm fine. Look, I need you to do something for me.'

'Of course,' she agreed, but then, before she let him move on, she added, 'Max, how are things?'

Bizarre. Confusing. 'I'm not sure,' he said honestly. 'I need time to find out. Can you clear my diary for the next two weeks?'

'I've done it,' she said, surprising him yet again. 'Well, I've shuffled what I can, and cleared most of it. I'm still waiting for Yashimoto to come back to me.'

Damn. He'd forgotten about Yashimoto. He was supposed to have been going on to Tokyo from New York to firm up the new contract.

'Maybe—'

'Max, I'll get him. It's not a problem. He can deal with Stephen—'

'No. Stephen doesn't know all the ins and outs. Get them both to call me—'

'Ma-ax?'

The warning voice from behind him made him turn, to find Jules propped up against the door frame cradling a cup of tea in her hands, one foot rested on the other, her bare toes looking curiously vulnerable. Not so her face. She was staring at him unflinchingly, and her expression was uncompromising. 'No phone calls,' she reminded him, a thread of steel that he'd forgotten about in her voice, and he gave a low groan of frustration and turned his back on her.

'OK. Scratch that, deal with him yourself, let Stephen handle it. I need to— Well, there are…'

'Rules?' Andrea said softly, and he sighed.

'Two weeks, no business, no distractions.'

'Well, hallelujah! I think I'm going to like your wife. I just hope I get the chance to meet her. Don't blow it, Max.'

Lord, what had happened to her? She was supposed to be on his side! 'I'll do my best,' he muttered. 'Look, I know it's against the rules, but if there really *is* a problem…'

'If there really is a problem I will, of

course, ring you. Give me your wife's number.'

'What?'

'You heard. I'll call her.'

'You don't need to trouble her.'

'No, I don't suppose I do, but I'll give her the veto.'

He said something rude, then apologised and handed the phone to Julia. 'She wants your number—for emergencies.'

'Right,' she said, and took the phone out of his hand and walked off with it, shutting the door behind her with her foot.

He swore again, scrubbed his hand through his hair and then heard a cry from the babies' room.

His daughters. That was what this was all about, he reminded himself, and, padding across the landing in bare feet, he went in there and lifted the one who was awake out of her cot and smiled at her.

Ava? He wasn't sure, so he said, 'Are you Ava?' out loud, and she turned her head and looked at the other cot.

'Libby?'

She turned back and beamed, reaching up and pulling his ear. Oh, well, it gave his nose a break. He shifted her slightly so she couldn't reach, and then sniffed. Hmm. She had a problem that was mercifully outside his experience, but that was fine. Jules wouldn't be long.

Would she?

'Max?'

'I'm in here,' he said, coming out of the babies' room with Libby in his arms. 'Are you happy now?'

'Mmm. She sounds nice. I've given her my number and my other contact details, just in case.'

'In case what? The office catches fire?'

'That would be pointless. What are you going to do, spit on it? Did you wake Libby?'

'No, she was awake. She—um—needs you.'

She chuckled and took the baby, kissing her and nuzzling her nose against her neck. 'Hello, monster. Is Daddy chicken?'

She started to cluck and squawk, and Libby thought it was hilarious and got the giggles, and she looked at Max over her head and saw his glower crumble and fade under the influence of Libby's delicious chuckles.

'Of course, part of the bonding process is learning about nappies,' she told him deadpan, and she could have sworn his colour drained a fraction. 'It's OK, I'll let you practise on a harmless one,' she said with a grin, and nearly laughed out loud when his shoulders dropped in relief.

He propped himself up in the doorway and watched her from a safe distance as she dealt with Libby, then she put the little girl back in his arms and washed her hands. Then she lifted Ava out and cuddled her while she found a clean nappy and got it ready, then changed her, too, and dropped the nappy in the bucket.

'Are those cloth nappies?' he asked, peering a little closer now it was safe.

She turned her head and raised an eyebrow at him. 'Don't look so shocked.'

'I—I'm not. I'm just surprised. I would have thought—I don't know; all that washing. You could just chuck disposables.'

'Mmm. Eight million a day, going into landfill.'

'*Eight million?* Good grief!'

'Mmm. Just in this country. And they don't biodegrade, either, so they're there for hundreds of years. Or I can wash these and dry them on the Aga. It's easier, cheaper and better, and they're not even made of cotton, they're made of bamboo. And they're lovely and soft. Right, Ava, that's you done!'

'How on earth do you manage both of them at once on your own?' he asked, looking utterly out of his depth, and she summoned a grin and shrugged.

'You learn coping strategies,' she said honestly. 'You deal with the urgent one first, and the other one gets to wait. It's normally Libby who waits, because Ava's got a shorter fuse.'

'So she's learned to manipulate you already?' he said, sounding astonished for the second time in as many minutes, which made her laugh out loud.

'Of course.' She gave him a dry look. 'She takes after you.'

His head jerked back and he eyed her doubtfully. 'I'm not sure that's a compliment.'

She chuckled. 'It's not. But babies are amazing. They're such good little survivors, and it doesn't take them long to sort out a pecking order. They'll have you sussed in no time flat, you wait and see. Right, girls, time for breakfast.'

'Not more of that disgusting goo,' he pleaded, looking appalled.

'No. They have instant multi-grain porridge for breakfast, and fruit. That's good and messy. I'll let you clean them up.'

He looked horrified, and she nearly laughed again. But then she remembered that any normal father of eight-month-old babies would *know* what their children had for breakfast, and

how to change a nappy, and that they were ma-
nipulative and very good at engineering the
adults around them.

Except, of course, that Max hadn't had the
chance, and that was her fault.

Turning away so he didn't see the thoughtful
frown on her face, she headed downstairs with
Ava, leaving him to follow with Libby. And, if
she was really lucky, she'd be able to get
through breakfast without drooling over the
sight of him in that robe which showed alto-
gether too much of those toned, muscular legs.
Not to mention the fact that she knew only too
well just how little he'd have on underneath it.

And it was absolutely nothing to do with her.
Not now, and not ever again, unless they could
turn this situation around and find a way to get
the two of them back together. Still, at least
he'd phoned his PA, as instructed.

She sounded sensible. Nice. Decent, and
utterly on her side. She was looking forward to
meeting her—but not yet. There was a lot of
ground to cover before they reached that point,
and she was going to make damn sure they
walked over every single inch of it.

'Right, girls, want some breakfast?'

* * *

He had to learn the hard way, of course, not to put the bowl close enough for Libby to slap her little hand in.

And then there was catching it before she had time to rub it in her hair. And on his face when he leant in to clean her up. Oh, boy, he'd need a shower by the time they were finished.

'Here.'

He looked up and took a warm, damp cloth from Jules, smiled his thanks and wondered where to start.

'Move the bowl,' she offered, and he pulled it out of reach and swiped most of the gloop off Libby's hand before she could stick it anywhere else, conscious of Jules hovering in range just in case he couldn't manage.

'Right, monster, let's try again,' he said, putting the cloth out of reach on the edge of the sink and settling down with the bowl and spoon. 'Open wide.'

He got most of it into her before she decided she'd had enough and spat it out at him with a cheerful grin, and he closed his eyes and laughed in exasperation before getting up, rinsing out the cloth and tackling her mucky little face.

Which she hated, apparently, because she

screamed the place down until he stopped, then beamed again.

'You're a madam,' he told her, grabbing her sticky hands and sorting them out one by one, and she giggled and tried to squirm out of the chair.

'What now?' he asked Jules.

'Bath time.'

'Bath—?' He rolled his eyes and sighed. 'Sounds messy.'

'It is. I'll let you do it.'

'Bathe them?' he asked, feeling a little flicker of panic.

'You'll cope,' she assured him drily, but he wasn't sure. He had a horrible feeling it was just another opportunity for him to make an idiot of himself or do something else wrong.

'I'll get dressed,' he said, and she laughed.

'I shouldn't bother. You'll probably get soaked.'

And her mouth twitched, and he realised she was enjoying this. Hugely.

He clamped his teeth together to hold back the retort, carried Libby upstairs and stopped by the bathroom door. 'So now what?'

'Put her on the floor on her tummy so she can practise crawling, and run the bath. Here, you can have Ava, too. I'll go and find some clothes for them. Don't undress them yet, though. They'll get cold waiting for you.'

Cold? How could they possibly get cold? The bathroom was steaming. But they were just little people. What did he know? He'd nearly scalded Ava last night. He wasn't going to argue.

Run the bath, he thought, and remembered something from his mother's wisdom: run the cold first, so the bath never has just hot in it.

Wise woman.

He ran the cold, then turned the hot tap on and swished it about until he thought it was hot enough. Was it? Hell, he wasn't going to risk another scald. He turned the hot off. Hmm. Maybe.

'Ava? What are you doing?'

He rescued the loo brush from her before she stuck it in her mouth and pointed her in the other direction, then yelled, 'I've run the bath.'

'Is it hot?'

'No!' he retorted with only a trace of sarcasm, and he heard her chuckle.

'Undress them, then. I'll be in in a second.'

So he undressed Ava, as she was heading for the brush again, and then Libby, and then he put her back down on the bath mat, rescued Ava yet again from the corner by the loo, and lowered her carefully into the water.

And yanked her out again instantly when she let out a piercing yell.

'What *now*?' Jules had flown into the room and snatched her from him, shielding her in her arms and glaring at him like a lioness defending her cub. 'I thought you said it wasn't hot!'

'It isn't!'

She bent over and touched the water, then shook her head and laughed weakly, sitting down on the side of the bath and shaking her head. 'No. You're right; poor little mite. It's freezing.'

'Freezing?'

'Mmm.'

Freezing. He sighed. 'I didn't want—'

'To burn them?' Her smile faded. 'OK. I'm sorry. I just thought it was common sense.'

'Well, clearly I haven't got any,' he retorted, sick of the whole business and wondering what he was going to do wrong next, but she took pity on him.

'Max, you're doing fine. Here, look, use the inside of your wrist. It should feel comfortable—not hot or cold. That's the best test.'

Hell. He was never going to survive this fortnight.

Never mind the rest of his life.

'How can it be so hard?' he grumbled gently,

retrieving Libby this time from the loo brush and plopping her in the bath beside her sister. 'Fourteen-year-old girls manage it.'

'No, they don't. They manage to get pregnant, but they don't manage to look after babies without support and coaching and lots of encouragement. Having ovaries doesn't make you a good mother, and not knowing how to run a bath doesn't make you a bad father. You'll get there, Max,' she added softly.

And he swallowed hard and looked away, because they were kneeling side by side, their shoulders brushing, and every now and then she swayed against him and her hip bumped his, and all he could think about was dragging her up against him and kissing her soft, full lips...

'Ow!'

Jules laughed and detached Libby's fingers from his hair, and the scent of her skin drifted across his face and nearly pushed him over the brink.

'Right, what next?' he asked, and forced himself to concentrate on the next instalment of his parentcraft class.

Eventually they were washed, dried and dressed in little denim dungarees and snugly warm jumpers, and Jules declared that as soon as he was dressed himself they were going out for a walk as it was a lovely day.

'Can they walk?' he asked, and she rolled her eyes.

'Of course not. We'll take the buggy.'

Obviously. Of course they couldn't walk. They could barely crawl. Except towards the loo brush. He put it on the window sill out of reach while he thought about it, and had a quick shower to get the baby breakfast out of his hair. And eyes. And nose.

Then he threw on his clothes and went down to the kitchen to join them. 'Right, are we all set?'

She eyed him thoughtfully. 'Jeans?'

'You know I don't own jeans,' he said, and then gave a short sigh when she rolled her eyes. 'What? What, for God's sake? Is it a character flaw that I don't own jeans?'

'No,' she said softly. 'It's a character flaw that you don't *need* to own jeans.'

He worked out the difference eventually, and scowled at her. 'Well, I don't—either own them, or need them.'

'Oh, you need them, of course you do. How are you going to crawl around the floor with the girls and the dog in your hand-tailored Italian suit-trousers?'

He stared down at his legs. Were they? He

supposed they were, and, when she put it like that, it did sound ridiculous. 'We could go and buy some,' he suggested.

'Good idea.'

'And while we're in town we can go to the Mercedes garage and talk about changing the car for something a little more baby-friendly.'

'There's nothing wrong with my car, and, anyway, it's John's!'

'Not yours,' he explained patiently. 'Mine.'

She swivelled her head and stared out of the window at his car. 'But Max—you love it,' she said softly.

He shrugged. 'So? I need a baby-carrier, Jules. No matter what happens with us, I need a baby-carrier. So I might as well do something about it now. And there's no room at the apartment for more than one car, so it'll have to go.'

'You could leave it here. Take mine when you have the girls.'

'I thought it was Blake's car?'

She frowned. 'Oh. Um—yes, it is,' she agreed. 'So I can't really let you have it.'

'So it's back to plan A.'

She looked at his car and chewed her lip doubtfully. She'd never driven it—never driven any of his sports cars. She'd had a little city car when he'd met her, and she'd hardly used it, so she'd sold it when they'd moved in together and she hadn't bought another one.

But she knew how much he loved it. It would be such a shame if he had to get rid of it. 'Or plan C,' she suggested. 'You buy another one, and leave it here for when you come up.'

He stared at her, then looked away to conceal his expression, because he'd suddenly realised they were talking as if she was going to be staying here, and he was going back to London without them.

And he didn't like it one bit.

They bought the jeans and some casual shoes and a couple of jumpers in one of the high-street department stores, and he emerged from the changing room looking stiff and uncomfortable and utterly gorgeous. 'Better?' he asked, a touch grumpily, and she smiled.

'Much. Right, let's go and sort the car out.'

They did. It was easy, because they had an ex-demonstration model which he could have instantly, and he held his hand out. 'Phone?'

'It's at home. But I've got Andrea's number in mine, if you want to call her to get the car on cover.'

He rolled his eyes and took her phone, made the call and handed it back in disgust. The negotiations complete, the salesman handed him the keys, and they headed back to the house in convoy, her with the babies, him alone in his new and very alien acquisition.

He followed her into the house and held out his hand again.

'So—my phone?'

She smiled a little guiltily. 'It's fine. You don't need it.'

'I might.'

'What for?'

'Apart from calling Andrea just now to get the car on cover—emergencies?'

'What—like contacting one of your business associates to set up a new deal, or checking that one of your overpaid and undervalued team is doing his or her job?'

'They aren't undervalued!' he protested, but she just arched a brow and stared straight back at him until he backed down. 'OK,' he sighed. 'So I have delegation issues.'

'Hallelujah!' she said, sounding so like Andrea that it made him want to strangle them both—or do something to ensure that they never spoke to each other again! 'So, anyway, you don't need your phone.'

'But what if there *is* an emergency?'

'Like what?'

He shrugged. 'I don't know. Like I set fire to the house or fall over on you all and squash you or drop one of the babies down the stairs—'

She went pale. 'Use the house phone.'

'What if we're out like we were this morning?' he pushed, the empty pocket in his jeans making him feel nervous and a little panicky.

'I'll have my mobile. You can use that. It's always in my bag.'

His eyes slid to the bag, just there on the side in the kitchen. It hadn't moved since he'd arrived last night, apart from to go to town with them, and, now he knew her phone was in it, the temptation to borrow it and sneak down the garden and make a couple of calls was overwhelming. Except, of course, he didn't have the contact numbers.

'Max, get over it,' she said firmly, and he realised there was no way he was going to talk her round. He swallowed hard and told himself Andrea would ring when she needed him. Except that he'd forgotten to tell her…

'Max, let it go. Andrea said she'd ring if it

was urgent.' And then she added curiously, 'What's she like? She sounded nice.'

He smiled at that, a little wryly. 'I don't know if I'd call her "nice". She's fifty-three, slim and elegant, and frighteningly efficient; she rules me with a rod of iron. You'll probably love her, but it's not like having you there, Jules. It was great working with you. You just knew what I wanted all the time and it was there, ready. I hardly had to think the thought, and sometimes I didn't even need to do that. I miss you.'

'I'm not coming back just because your new PA isn't as good as me,' she retorted, but his mouth quirked and he shook his head.

'Oh, she's good, but at the end of the day, when we've finished work, she doesn't look at me like you did,' he said, his voice lower. 'As if she wants to rip my clothes off. And I don't undress her in the shower and make love to her up against the tiles until the security staff wonder who the hell's being murdered because of all the screaming.'

She felt a tide of colour sweep over her at that, and shook her head. 'Max, stop it. It was only once.'

'And it was amazing,' he said softly, and, reaching out his hand, he cupped her flushed cheek and lifted her chin, as his mouth came down and found hers in a gentle, tender kiss that could so easily lead to…

She stepped back, her legs like jelly. 'Max, no! Stop it.'

He straightened up, his eyes burning, and gave a crooked smile. 'Sorry,' he murmured, but he didn't look in the least bit sorry. He looked like the cat that got the cream, and she could have screamed with frustration.

'So—how about that walk we were going to have?' he said, which just showed what he knew about babies and their timetabling.

'The girls need lunch and a nap, and so do I. We can go for a walk later if it's still nice.'

'What am I supposed to do, then?' he asked. She realised he was utterly at a loss with so much unstructured time on his hands, and she gave a wicked little smile.

'You could wash the nappies.'

He'd never gone in her handbag.

It was one of those unwritten rules, like swearing in front of ladies and leaving the seat up, that his mother had drummed into him as a child.

But, with the house quiet and all of them asleep, he stood, arms folded, and stared at her bag. It was only the phone. Just one call. He could sneak down the garden, or out to the car, and she'd never know.

He could even see the corner of it, sticking up out of the pile of junk that she seemed to have in it. And that was a change. Her bag had always been immaculately well organised before, and now it was a walking skip.

With a phone in it.

He caught the corner of it gingerly between finger and thumb and lifted it out of the bag as if it would bite him. It was a very ordinary phone, and he knew how to use it because he'd made a call on it this afternoon. And he knew Andrea's number was in there. He had to talk to her, he told himself, trying to justify it.

He had to.

He went into the address book and then, on impulse, he scrolled down to M, and there he was: Max, and his mobile number. And the apartment. And work. He looked under ICE— in case of emergency—and found his numbers all repeated.

In her new phone.

Because of the girls, he reminded himself, squashing the leap of hope, and then had a thought. If he rang his mobile number, it would ring, and he'd be able to find it…

* * *

What on earth?

She lifted her head, stared at the pillow and pulled it aside.

Max's phone was ringing—on silent, because she'd silenced it, but the vibration had alerted her. And the number that had come up was her mobile.

Which was in her handbag.

'You're cheating,' she said into it, and there was a muttered curse and he cut the connection. Suppressing a smile, she threw back the covers and slipped out of bed, pulled on her jeans and jumper, ran her fingers through her hair and went downstairs.

He was standing by the bag, her phone in hand, looking defiant and guilty all at once, and she felt suddenly sorry for him, plunged head-first into this bizarre situation that was totally outside his experience, dislocated from everything that was familiar.

Except her, and even she'd changed beyond recognition, she realised.

She smiled. 'It's OK, Max, I'm not going to bite.'

'Just nag me.'

'No. Not even nag you. I'm going to ask you, one more time, to take this seriously. To give it your best shot, to see if we can make a go of it. If not for us, then for the girls.'

He swallowed hard, and looked away. 'I need to make a call, Jules. There's something important I forgot to tell Andrea.'

'Is anyone going to die?'

He looked startled. 'Of course not.'

'Or be hurt?'

'No.'

'So it doesn't really matter.'

'It'll just hold things up a few days until they realise.'

'Realise?'

'There's a document I was going to get faxed to Yashimoto.'

'And he won't ask Stephen or Andrea for it?'

He shrugged. 'I don't know.'

'So what's the worst that will happen? You'll lose a few thousand?'

'Maybe more.'

'Does it matter? I mean, it's not as if you're strapped, Max. You don't ever have to work again if you don't want to. A few pounds, a few days out of a lifetime, isn't so much to ask, is it?'

He turned slowly back to her, his eyes bleak. 'I thought we had it all. I thought we were happy.'

'We were—but it all just got too much, Max. And I'm not going back to it, so if you can't do this, can't learn to delegate and take time out to enjoy your family, then we don't have a future. And, to have a future, we have to be able to trust each other.'

He didn't move for a moment, but then he sighed softly, threw her phone back into her bag and straightened up.

'You'd better show me how to work the washing machine, then, hadn't you?' he said with a little twisted smile, and she felt the breath ease out of her lungs.

'It'll be a pleasure,' she said, almost giddy with relief, and, leading him into the utility room, she introduced him to the concept of home laundry.

CHAPTER FOUR

THE babies were cute.

Sweet, messy, temperamental and cute. And *boring*.

Not when they were awake, but when they were asleep, and Jules was asleep, and the house was so quiet he wanted to scream.

And it struck him he was the one doing all the adjusting.

How fair was that? Not fair at all, he thought, simmering, and it hadn't been his idea that he'd been cut out of their lives.

So far—thirty-odd hours in—he'd learned to run a bath the right temperature, how to put the washing machine on, how to aim food at a baby's face, not always successfully, and how not to drink tea. That had been lesson one, and one he was unlikely ever to forget.

But now, at eleven o'clock at night, when he would usually be working on for at least another three hours, Julia had gone to bed, the babies were settled till the morning and there was nothing to do.

Nothing on the television, no way of keeping in touch with Yashimoto—who would by then have been back in the office, because he started early—and no way of contacting anyone in New York, where they'd all still be at work.

He paced around the kitchen, made tea, threw it down the sink, because he'd drunk gallons of the stuff during the day, and contemplated the wine he'd brought back the night before from the pub. He'd only had a couple of glasses, so there was nearly two bottles, but he didn't drink alone. Dangerous.

Then he thought of the pub.

He stepped out of the back door to let Murphy out into the garden, and coincidentally see if the pub lights were on, and realised it was in darkness. Of course it was, he thought in disgust. It was a gastro-pub in the country—a restaurant, really, more than a pub—and they stopped serving at something ridiculous like nine, so he couldn't even go there and drown his sorrows. And it was so damned *quiet*!

Except for that screaming he could hear in the background. He'd heard it a moment ago, and now he was standing outside the French doors he could hear it clearly, a truly blood-curdling noise, and it chilled him to the bone. Murphy's hackles were up and he was growling softly, so Max called him back inside and shut the door, then went upstairs and knocked on Julia's bedroom door. She opened it a moment later, wearing pyjamas with cats all over them and rumpled with sleep, and he had to force himself to stick to the point.

'There's a noise,' he said without preamble, not letting himself look at the little cats running about all over her body. 'Screaming. I think someone's being attacked.'

She cocked her head on one side, listened, and then smiled. 'It's a badger,' she said. 'Or a fox. They both scream at night. I'm not sure which is which, but at this time of year I think it's probably a badger. The foxes make more noise in the spring. Did it wake you?'

And then she looked at him and sighed. 'Oh, Max—you haven't been to bed yet, have you? You ought to sleep. You're exhausted.'

'I'm not exhausted. I'm never asleep at this time of night.'

'Well, you should be,' she scolded softly, then went back into her bedroom and emerged again, stuffing her arms into a fluffy robe that hid the cats, to his disappointment. 'Tea?'

He didn't want tea. The last thing he wanted was tea, but he would have drunk neat acid just then to have her company.

'Tea sounds great,' he said gruffly, and followed her downstairs.

It couldn't be easy for him, to be lobbed in at the deep end, and it didn't get much deeper than twins. He'd never been someone who needed much sleep, and, with nothing to do in the night but think, he must be turning this whole situation over and over in his mind.

Good, she told herself. Maybe he'd see the error of his ways.

Or maybe she'd just drive him away.

'Is there any wood on the fire?' she asked, and he shrugged.

'I don't know. There was. I put the guard up—does it stay alight all night?'

'I don't normally light it,' she confessed. 'The girls and I spend most of our time in the kitchen.'

'So why did you ask?'

'Because I thought—I've got DVDs of the girls, right from when they were born. Actually, from before. I've got a 4D-DVD of the scan. It's amazing.'

'4D?'

'Mmm—3D and real time. They call it 4D. You can see them moving, and it's amazingly real. And I've got lots of stuff of them when they were in special care, and all the things they do for you, like hand- and footprints and their tiny little name-bands and weight charts and stuff like that. I thought, if it was warm in there, we could watch them, but you'll probably think it's all really boring—'

'No! No, I won't. I—I'd like to see,' he said gruffly, sounding curiously unlike Max, uncertain and hesitant. He was never hesitant, and she looked at him searchingly.

'Good,' she said softly. 'Go and see if you can revive the fire, and I'll bring us tea.'

And biscuits, some rather gorgeous chocolate biscuits that were more chocolate than biscuit, and some cheese and crackers, because she knew he'd be hungry and he frankly needed fattening up.

He was crouching by the fire when she went in, blowing on the embers and trying to breathe life into the glowing remains, and as she put the tray down the logs flickered to life and a lovely orange glow lit the hearth.

'Oh, that's super. Well done. Here, have some cheese and biscuits,' she instructed, and rummaged in the cupboard next to the television for the DVDs.

'Scan first?' she suggested, and his brows pulled down slightly, as if he was troubled.

He nodded, and she slipped it into the slot and sat back against the front of the sofa by his legs, cradling her tea in her hands while the images of the unborn babies unrolled in front of them.

'How pregnant were you when this was taken?' he asked softly, a little edge in his voice that she'd never heard before, and she swivelled round and looked up at him, puzzled.

'Twenty-six weeks.'

A shadow went over his face, and he pressed his lips together and stared at the screen as if his life depended on it. She turned back and watched it with him, but she was deeply conscious of a tension in him that she'd never felt before. When the DVD was finished and she took it out, she felt the tension leave him, and, as he leant back against the sofa to drink his tea, his hand shook a little.

Odd. Max's hands never shook. Ever.

Under any circumstances. And yet he'd always been so adamant that he didn't want children, that their lives were complete without them. So why had the images of his children before they were born been so moving to him?

The fire was roaring away now, and Murphy heaved himself up from his position in front of it and came over, flopping down against Max's legs. Max leant down and scratched the dog's neck and pulled his ears, an absent expression on his face, and Murphy lifted his head and gazed adoringly at Max as if he'd just found his soulmate.

'I think you've got a new friend,' she said, and Max gave a crooked little grin and smoothed Murph's head with a gentle hand.

'Apparently so. I expect he misses John.'

'I expect he wants the crackers on your plate,' she said pragmatically, and Max chuckled and the mood lifted a fraction, and she breathed a little easier.

'So—what's next?' he asked, and she put on the first film of the girls after they'd been born.

'Here they are—they're two days old. They were born at thirty-three weeks, because my uterus was having trouble expanding because of the scarring and they'd stopped growing. Jane and Peter came in and filmed it for me. They were amazing—so supportive.'

'I would have been supportive,' he said, his voice rough, and she felt another stab of guilt.

'I didn't know that, Max. You'd always been so against the idea of children. If I even so much as mentioned IVF you flew off the handle. How was I to know you wanted to be involved?'

'You could have asked me. You could have given me the choice.'

She could have. She could have, but she hadn't, and it was too late now to change it. But she could apologise, she realised, and she turned towards him and took his hand.

'I'm really sorry,' she said, making herself meet his eyes and steeling herself for the anger that she knew she'd see in them. But instead of anger there was pain. 'Max?' she whispered, and he pulled his hand away and stood up.

'Maybe we'll do this another time,' he said, and without a word he headed for the door. She heard him go upstairs; heard the bathroom door close and water running. With a sigh she turned off the DVD player and the television, put the fire-guard up and cleared away their cups and plates, then put Murphy out one last time before shutting him in the kitchen and going upstairs.

She heard the shower turn off as she went into her own bedroom and closed the door, then a few minutes later she heard him come out of the bathroom and go down the landing to his bedroom, closing the door with a soft click.

She didn't sleep for hours, and, when she woke, it was to hear the back door open and Max calling the dog. The sky was just light, the day barely started, and, as she lifted herself up on one elbow, she saw Max heading down the drive with Murphy trotting beside him. He was wearing jogging bottoms and trainers with a T-shirt, and she watched him turn out onto the hill, cross the river and run away up through the village out of sight, the dog at his heels.

She didn't know what was wrong, but she had a feeling it wasn't the obvious. There just seemed to be something else going on, something she didn't know about, and she didn't know if she could ask.

Probably not. He'd been pretty unapproachable last night. Maybe he'd tell her in his own good time, but one thing was absolutely certain.

Max was right out of his comfort zone, and living with him for the next two weeks was going to be interesting, to say the least.

Not to mention frustrating and heartbreaking and undoubtedly painful.

She just hoped it would prove to be worth it...

He ran along the lane out of the village, turned left along another tiny, winding lane, cut down across a field and over the river on a flat iron bridge—used by tractors, he supposed—and then up to a bridlepath that cut through to the village again just opposite the drive to Rose Cottage.

It had taken twenty minutes, so he supposed it was about three miles. Not far enough to numb him, but enough to take the edge off it and distract him from the endless turmoil in his mind.

The light was on in the kitchen as he jogged across the drive, and Jules was watching him, her face unreadable at that distance through the old leaded lights. But she had her arms full of washing or something, and she was in that fluffy dressing-gown again, presumably with the little cats underneath.

He suppressed a groan and walked the last few steps to the back door and let himself in, a wet and muddy Murphy by his side.

'Bed!' she ordered, and the dog turned and went into his bed in the space under the stairs.

'Is that just him, or do I have to go in there, too?' Max asked, and she smiled a little uncertainly and searched his face with troubled eyes.

'Are you all right?'

'Fine. We've had a good run—'

She stopped him with her hand on his arm and looked up into his eyes with that way of hers that made him feel uncomfortable and vulnerable. 'Are you really all right?'

'I'm fine,' he said, a little more sincerely, because he was, really. It was just that DVD which had stirred things up, made him sad and emotional all over again, and he hated it. Hated being out of control of his feelings—hated his feelings, full stop.

'I've made tea,' she said, and he opened his mouth to tell her he didn't want any damn tea, then shut it, smiled and nodded.

'Thanks. Are the babies awake yet?'

She shook her head. 'No. They will be soon. Why?'

'Oh, just wondered. I need a shower, but I don't want to disturb them. I'll have my tea and wait a bit, if you can stand me all sweaty and mud-splattered.'

She ran her eyes over him and gave a tiny huff of laughter, but, as she turned away, he noticed a soft brush of colour in her cheeks. Really? He could still do that to her?

'I'm sure I can stand you for long enough to drink your tea,' she said lightly, but her voice was a little strange, not quite itself, and she was folding and smoothing nappies on top of the Aga as if her life depended on it.

He thought of their kiss, just the lightest touch of his lips to hers, and heat seared through him. Because he wanted to do it again, wanted to haul her up against him and tunnel his fingers through that tousled, rumpled hair, and plunder her mouth with his until she was whimpering with need and clawing at him for more...

'On second thoughts, maybe I'll go and have a look through my clothes and find something to wear after my shower,' he said, and retreated to the door before he embarrassed himself.

'What's wrong with yesterday's new clothes?' she asked, and he hesitated in the doorway, one foot on the bottom of the stairs just outside in the hall, and looked at her over his shoulder.

'Nothing. I just wasn't sure if I they'd be right for what we're doing today.'

'So what are we doing?' she asked, looking puzzled.

Good question. 'Taking the girls to the seaside,' he told her, thinking on his feet. 'It's a gorgeous day, and the forecast is mild and sunny all day.'

'In which case your jeans and jumper will be perfect. Come back and sit down and drink your tea. If you start banging about in the room next to them, they *will* wake up, at this time of day, and frankly the peace is short-lived enough.'

He swallowed, crushed the lust that was threatening to give him away. But he needn't have worried because she scooped up the washing and carried it out to the utility room, and he took his tea over to the sofa in the bay window and sat down with one foot hitched up on the other knee, and by the time she came back in he had himself back under control.

Just.

He was right, it was a gorgeous day.

They took the babies to Felixstowe, parked the car at one end of the prom and walked all the way along to the other end. The wind was from the north-west, so they were totally sheltered by the low cliffs at the north end. But, when they turned back into the wind, it was a little cooler so Max turned the buggy round and towed it, while she walked beside him and enjoyed the freedom of being able to swing her arms as she walked.

'Do you know,' she pointed out, 'that, apart from corporate trips when we've been abroad, this is the first time in six years that we've been to the beach?'

He glanced sideways at her and pulled a face. 'I suppose you're right. It's not something I've ever thought of doing—not in England, anyway. And I've never been a beach-holiday person.'

'I'm not talking about beach holidays,' she said. 'I'm talking about walking by the sea, with a good, stiff breeze tugging my hair and the taste of salt on my skin. It's gorgeous—bracing and healthy and—oh, wonderful!'

And then she looked at him, and saw him watching her with something very familiar and deeply disturbing in his eyes, and she coloured and turned away quickly. 'Oh look—there's a ship coming in,' she said, which was ridiculous because there had been lots, but she caught his smile out of the corner of her eye and the breath stuck in her throat.

He had no right doing that to her—bringing back so many memories with just one slow, lazy smile. They might not have walked on the beach, but they'd made love many, many times on their roof terrace overlooking the Thames, with the smell of the river drifting up to them and the salty tang in the air. And she could tell, just from that one glance, that he was remembering it as well.

'I'll just make sure the babies are all right,' she said hastily, and, going round to the other side of the buggy, she tucked them up and then followed behind, staring at his shoulders as he towed the babies and strolled along with the air of a man who did it every day of the week.

Just like a real father, with a wife and two beautiful children, not a pressed man who'd been forced to submit to some bonding time with his newly discovered infants.

Oh, what a mess.

Would they ever get out of it?

'Jules?'

She realised she'd stopped, and he'd stopped, too, and had turned to look at her, his eyes troubled.

He let go of the buggy and came round to her side. 'What's wrong?'

She shrugged, unable to speak, and with a little sigh he put his arms round her and eased her against his chest.

'Hey, it'll be all right,' he murmured, but she wasn't so sure. It was less than two days, and he'd already broken the rules by stealing her phone and trying to find his. Goodness knows what else he'd do while her back was turned. He was up half the night—could he be using her phone?

Did she care? So long as he was there in the day and trying, did it matter if he cheated?

Yes!

Or—no, not really, so long as he learned the work-life balance lesson?

'Come on, let's go and get a coffee. There's a little café I noticed near the car. I've brought drinks for the girls, and maybe they can warm up their jars.'

'Gloop?' he said, looking wary, and she thought of his new jumper and smiled.

'It's OK, I'll feed them, if you like,' she promised. 'I'll just let you pay.'

'It'll be a pleasure,' he said with a sigh of relief, and, going back to the other side of the buggy, he towed it the rest of the way to the car without a murmur.

The babies were ready for bed early that night.

'It must be the sea air,' Jules said as she heated

their supper—pots of home-made food this time, he noticed, and wondered if it was better for them.

'Does that have all the right nutrients in it?' he asked, and she stared at him as if he was mad.

'It's food—not a chemical formula. Roast chicken, broccoli, carrots, roast potatoes, gravy made with stock—of course it's got all the right nutrients.'

'And you cooked it?'

'Well, of course I cooked it!' she said with an exasperated sigh. 'Who else?'

He shrugged. 'Sorry. It's just—I hardly ever saw you cook, and I don't think you ever did a roast.'

'No, of course not. We never had that long to do something so unimportant—'

'Jules, stop it! I was just—'

'What? Criticising the way I'm looking after my children?'

'They're my children, too!'

'So learn how to cook for them,' she said crossly, and threw a cookery book at him. 'Here you go. There's chicken breast, mince, salmon steaks, prawns and pork chops in the freezer. Take your pick. You can do supper for us while I get the girls in bed.'

And, stalking off with one of them in each arm, she left him sitting there staring blankly at the book.

Jeez. He could make coffee and toast and scrambled eggs, at a push. And he could unwrap stuff and shove it in the microwave, or pick up the phone and order.

But—cook? Real ingredients? Hell's teeth, he hadn't done that for years. Fifteen years? Not since…

He opened the book and flicked through the pages. What was it they'd had in the pub? Chicken breast stuffed with brie and wrapped in bacon, or something like that. She'd given him cheese last night—not brie, but cheddar. Would that do? Maybe. And how about bacon?

He stepped over the dog and investigated the fridge.

No bacon. No brie, either, come to that, and very little cheddar.

But there was pesto, and he thought he'd seen some pasta in the store cupboard in the kitchen when she'd been rummaging for biscuits.

So—pasta with chicken and pesto? A few toasted pine-nuts and a bag of salad…

No salad. Probably no pine nuts.

Peppers?

He hauled out a few things he'd seen served with similar dishes, set them all on the kitchen table and settled down with them to try and find a recipe that tied at least some of them in. Then, having found one, he had to work out how to use the microwave and, worse, how to use the Aga. Or even find the tools to reach that point.

Starting with a sharp knife, and a chopping board, and a deep, heavy pan. That was what the instructions said.

He found them, thawed and sliced the chicken, fried it in the pan with olive oil, onion and peppers, opened the pesto—and discovered mould.

Damn!

But there was rice, too, and prawns, so—how about paella? How the hell did you make paella?

He turned back to the book, wondering how long, exactly, Jules could remove herself from the kitchen. Long enough for him to ruin every single ingredient!

Simple. He'd order something in. Even she couldn't object to him doing that on the house phone.

Except he was supposed to be doing this

himself, and rising to a challenge wasn't something that normally held him back. So—paella. How hard could it be?

'Oh! Risotto?' she said hesitantly, poking it and sniffing.

'Paella,' he corrected. 'The pesto was off.'

'Oh, it would be. There's a new one in the cupboard.'

He rolled his eyes and sighed. 'Right. Well, I was adaptable,' he said, sounding pleased with himself, and she sniffed again.

'How much garlic did you use?'

'I don't know. It said two cloves. It seemed a lot, so I only used one.'

'Clove, or bulb?'

He frowned in confusion. 'What's the difference?'

'Um—the bulb is the whole thing, a silvery-white papery thing with bumps and a stalk in the middle. A clove is one of the little bits inside.'

He scowled and turned away. 'Well, you should have been here if you're going to complain.'

'Hey, I haven't complained.'

'You haven't tasted it yet.'

'Well, so it might be a bit garlicky. So what? I'm not going to kiss anyone, am I?' she said, and then wished furiously that she could repossess her words, because he turned slowly and studied her.

'It could be arranged,' he murmured, his eyes dragging slowly over her as if he was trying to peel away her clothes.

'In your dreams,' she muttered, and took out two bowls. 'Here—dish up. I'll get us a drink. Do you want some of that wine?'

'I wouldn't mind the white. The red could be a bit heavy.'

'Oh, I don't know,' she said wickedly. 'It might balance the garlic.'

Foolish girl. He threw the spoon back into the pan and stalked off into the hall, disappearing out of the front door and slamming it behind him, shrugging on his jacket as he went.

Oops. That had been mean of her to tease him. She knew he couldn't cook, and he'd done his best. And, apart from the garlic and the fact that it was a bit over-cooked, it looked fine.

His car—the sports car, the silly, fast, dangerous one—shot off the drive in a spray of gravel, and she sighed and covered the pan, pulled it to the side and sat down to wait. Either he'd come back, she thought, in which case she'd apologise, or he wouldn't, in which case—

What? She'd lost the girls their father, and

herself the only man she'd ever loved, just for the sake of keeping her sassy mouth shut?

Oh, damn. And she couldn't even phone him to apologise.

CHAPTER FIVE

HE HIT the M25 before he saw sense, and he came off at the first junction, pulled up in the tatty, run-down service area, cut the engine and slammed his hands down on the steering wheel.

What the hell was he doing? She'd been *teasing* him! That was all. Nothing drastic. She'd always teased him, but he'd forgotten. Forgotten all sorts of things. What it felt like to hold her, what it felt like to touch her, to bury himself inside her—

He swallowed hard. No. He couldn't let himself think about that. It was too soon; he was way off being allowed that close to her. But he wanted her, wanted to touch her, to hold her, to feel her warmth.

God, he was *lonely*. So damned lonely without her.

So he couldn't do this, couldn't throw in the towel, give up on his beautiful little girls and run away, because she'd teased him about the bloody garlic!

With a shaky sigh, he started the engine, pulled out of the car park, shot back down the slip road onto the A12 and went back to his wife.

He wasn't coming back.

She'd sat in the window, huddled by the glass with a fleece wrapped round her shoulders and waited until the pub was shut, but there was still no sign of him.

What if he'd broken down? What if he'd gone off the road in a fit of temper? He seemed so angry these days, angrier than she'd ever seen him. Was that her fault? It must be. What else could it be?

And now he was who knew where, maybe lying upside down in a ditch full of water.

Lights sliced across the garden, blinding her with the glare of his headlamps as he turned in and cut the engine. The security lights came on as he got out of the car, and then she heard the car door slam and his feet crunch across the gravel as he approached the front door.

He paused and looked at her through the window, his face sombre, and then, with a slight shake of his head, he walked to the door, and she heard it open and close. Then he was there, filling the hall doorway with his brooding, silent presence.

'I'm sorry,' he said.

'No, I'm sorry,' she said, getting up and walking towards him, her foot a little stiff from sitting with it tucked under her for so long while she watched for him. 'I shouldn't have been so mean to you.'

'It's OK. It's not your fault,' he said gruffly. 'I overreacted.'

'No, you didn't. You were doing your best. I know you can't cook, and I should have given you more help, not just flung you in at the deep end and expected you to cope because you criticised me.'

'I didn't. Or, at least, I didn't mean to. I was just asking. I'm sorry if it came over as criticism.'

So many sorries. From Max? She shook her head slowly and went over to the Aga. 'Forget it. Have you eaten?'

'No. I was going home. I'd got to the M25 before I came to my senses.'

She frowned. 'That's fifty miles!'

'I know. I was— Well, let's just say it took a while for me to calm down. Which is ridiculous. So, in answer to your question, no, I haven't eaten, and yes, please, if it isn't ruined. Not that I think you could ruin it. I'd already done a fair job.'

'It'll be fine,' she told him, determined to eat it if it choked her. 'So, I believe I was going to pour you a glass of wine?'

He gave a choked laugh. 'That sounds good.'

'Red or white?'

He smiled, 'I'll finish the red. It'll balance the garlic,' he said with irony, and she smiled back and handed him the bottle and a glass. She turned back to the paella, taking the lid off and blinking at the smell, but she dished up without a word, and they sat down at the table and ate it in a slightly strained and civilised silence, until finally Max pushed it away and met her eyes.

'Bit heavy on the seasoning for me,' he said wryly, and she put her fork down and smiled with him.

'I'm not really hungry,' she lied. 'Shall I make some tea?'

'No. I'm fine with the wine, but I could do with some toast or something.'

'Cheese and biscuits? Or I might be able to find an apple pie in the freezer I could put in the oven?'

'Sounds nice. We can have it later, after the cheese and biscuits.'

She chuckled and cleared away the table, put the cheese and biscuits out and the apple pie in the oven, then got herself a glass and poured a little wine into it.

'Sorry, I didn't realise you wanted some.'

'It's OK. I don't usually, because I'm still feeding them, but tonight—well, I just thought I'd join you.'

'Feel free.'

She swirled it round in the glass, then met his eyes over the top of it. 'So—why were you so angry?' she asked tentatively. 'It wasn't just the garlic thing.'

He sighed sharply and ran his hand through his hair, then met her eyes again. 'I don't know, it's— Well, it's this place, really.'

'The cottage? It's lovely!'

'Oh, I'm sure, but I just hate the idea of it. You're my wife, Jules. I don't want you living in another man's house.'

She pulled back and leant against the chair, eyeing him over the table and wondering if she'd been a bit too quick to forgive. 'Isn't it fortunate, then, that it's nothing to do with you? Because we're happy here.'

'And you couldn't be happy in your own house?'

'You mean your own house?'

He sighed. 'No, yours. I'd buy you one—in your own name. God knows I owe you that, at the very least, if you won't come back to me. We're talking about housing my children, for heaven's sake.'

'I can house your children.'

'Yes, in someone else's house, living off his generosity! I don't like it, Jules. I don't like it at all. I don't like staying here, I don't like the idea that he could come back at any time and have the right to be here. I want privacy while we sort this out, and all the time I feel as if I'm waiting for the other shoe to drop.'

She studied him thoughtfully for a moment, then gave a gentle sigh. 'Well, then, perhaps it's just as well that you want to buy me a house, because he's coming back in a month and I'm going to be homeless.'

His eyes narrowed. 'You could always come back to me.'

'What, to the apartment? I hardly think so.'

'We could buy a house in London. Hampstead, or somewhere like that, or Barnes or Richmond—'

'Or I could stay here in Suffolk, near my friends.'

'You've got friends here?'

He sounded so shocked and surprised she nearly laughed. 'Well, of course I have. Jane and Peter, and I've made other friends, lots of them, through the hospital and the twins' support group, and the Real Nappy network—'

'The *what*?'

'The Real Nappy network. And there's a coffee group for young mums in the village which I go to.'

He stared at her as if she'd sprouted horns.

'So—you want to stay out here?'

'Yes. At least—until we know how it's going to go with us. I don't have any infra-structure in London, Max. I'd be so lonely there, and I know if we're in London you'll just be off all the time, popping into the office for a minute or whatever, and before I know what's what you'll be in New York or Tokyo or Sydney.'

'OK. So you want a house here. Are there any for sale?'

She did laugh at that. 'I have no idea, Max. I haven't been looking.'

'So what were you going to do?'

She looked down, her laughter dying. 'I'm not sure.' Go back to him? No. But tell him?

Contact him? Almost certainly, because not to do so was too unfair.

'How's the pie?'

'Oh. I don't know.'

She opened the oven and pulled it out; it was crisp and golden and full of the fragrance of apples. 'It's done.'

'So let's eat it, and worry about the house later.'

Hell. She wanted to stay out here, in the middle of Suffolk?

With her friends—friends he'd never met—friends he'd only heard about, because she'd hardly ever seen them, so he hadn't been able to track her down through them because he'd had no idea how to go about finding them.

She'd met up with Jane in town a few times, spent a weekend or two with her when they'd lived in Berkshire. He dimly remembered her saying they were moving, but not where to, just that it would be further. And, since he'd had no idea what Jane's surname was, that hadn't been a lot of help.

And they were more important to her than him?

No. Stop it. She hadn't said that. She'd simply said that, until they knew what was happening with them, she wanted to stay near her infrastructure.

Well, he could understand that. He felt pretty damn lost without his.

'Is it OK?'

He frowned. What?

'The pie—is it OK?'

The pie. He stared at his plate, almost empty, and realised he'd hardly tasted it. He blinked in surprise.

'Yes, it's fine. It's lovely. Thanks.'

'You were miles away.'

He gave her a crooked smile. 'Actually, no, I was right here, wondering what happens next,' he confessed.

'Next?'

'About the house, I mean.'

She stared at him for a second, then looked hastily away, soft colour invading her cheeks. 'Oh. Um—right. Well, I suppose I have to start looking.'

What on earth had she thought he was talking about? Unless…

No. She wasn't interested; she'd made that clear. She'd been giving out hands-off signals since he'd arrived, pretty much. Apart from that one stolen kiss that she'd stopped in its tracks, she hadn't so much as brushed against him except by accident.

So why was she blushing?

'We could look on the Internet,' she said, and he felt his radar leap to life.

'Internet?'

'Mmm—in the study. It's John's, but he's happy for me to use it. He emails me regularly, and I reply, telling him how things are and sending him photos of Murphy and the babies.'

The babies? She sent John Blake photos of his babies? And then he stopped thinking about John Blake and paid attention to the core business.

There was a computer in the house. A computer with Internet access. Which meant he could check his email, keep in touch with his colleagues and employees, and keep an eye on what was going on in the financial markets. Before he went completely insane from the lack of information.

'Good idea,' he said. 'Let's load the dishwasher and go and have a look.'

'Sure.'

She went over to the sink and scraped the remains of their meal down the sink into the waste-disposal unit, then turned back to get the rest of the things just as he arrived at her elbow with another plate and a pan.

'Whoops,' he said with a grin, shifting the pan out of the way before she collided with it, and instead she collided with his chest, her soft, full breasts squashing against him and her eyes flying up to meet his, wide and startled.

'Steady,' he murmured, putting the pan down on the side and setting the plate back onto the table, and then, suddenly reluctant to lose that soft, warm contact, he let his arms drift round her and drew her closer.

'Max?' she whispered, her voice little more than a breath. But it was enough—just that soft word telling him all he needed to know about how much she wanted him, and, without waiting for any further invitation, he lowered his head, closed his eyes and touched his mouth to hers.

She couldn't let him do this.

She couldn't…

She must taste of garlic. How he could tell after the paella, she didn't know, but she thought back to their row, to her comment that it didn't matter because nobody was going to kiss her.

But Max was kissing her as if his life depended on it—and suddenly she didn't care about the garlic, only about kissing him back, feeling the strength of his arms around her, the powerful thighs bracketing hers, the harsh sound of his breathing muffled against her face as he plundered her mouth with his, his lips and tongue urgent, his body hard against hers, trapping her between him and the sink so she was under no illusions about his reaction.

One hand slid round under her jumper and cradled her breast, and she whimpered softly. The sound caught in his mouth and echoed back to her in a deep, primitive groan that was dragged up from his boots.

'Jules, I need you,' he whispered harshly, his mouth tracking over her jaw, his teeth nipping her, not enough to hurt but just enough to drive her further over the edge. And then his tongue stroked over the tiny insult, soothing, tasting, his lips dragging softly over her skin and leaving fire in their wake.

He was driving her crazy, and he knew it, but she couldn't stop him. There was no way she could stop him, because she needed this every bit as much as he did.

Or so she thought, until the little voice clamouring at the back of her subconscious fought its way up to the surface and she realised that one of the babies was crying. Suddenly Max was shunted off the top of her list, and she felt the passion die away, replaced by the fundamental fact of her motherhood.

'Max,' she said, turning her head away, and he groaned and dropped his head onto her shoulder.

'No, Jules. Don't stop me, for God's sake, please.'

'The babies,' she said, and he went still for a second, then sighed heavily and eased away, slashes of colour on his cheekbones, his eyes dark with arousal as he stared down at her. His chest was heaving, and, after the longest moment, he closed his eyes and turned away.

'Go and sort them out,' he said. 'I'll wait for you.'

But she knew that would be the stupidest thing she could do.

'No, Max. I don't think that's a good idea. I'm going to go to bed.'

'No!'

'Yes. I'm sorry. It's not— We aren't ready yet.'

He gave a rude snort, and, without waiting for him to say another thing, she fled for the stairs.

'She's not ready, Murphy. What do you think of that?'

Murphy thumped his tail and gazed up at Max with adoring eyes, and he sighed and rubbed the dog's ears gently. 'Yeah, I quite agree. Rubbish, isn't it? What am I going to do if she's never ready, Murphs? This is driving me crazy. The whole damn situation's driving me crazy.'

He poured the last glass of wine out of the bottle and stared morosely at it. If only there was something to *do*!

Something more gripping than taking his wife to bed and making love to her until she was so desperate for him that she couldn't speak, couldn't breathe, couldn't do anything except scream and sob with need.

He swore, short and to the point, and, picking up the TV remote, he turned the set on and channel-hopped. Nothing. Even the news was dull, nothing to hold his interest, and he was on the point of hurling the handset through the window when Jules appeared in the doorway, dressed in her little cat-pyjamas and that fluffy dressing gown, her bare feet sticking out of the bottom and looking vulnerable and appealing.

He wanted to kiss them, take each toe in his mouth and suck it slowly.

'Is it safe to come in?'

He gave a rough sigh. 'Yes, it's safe. I'm sorry. It's just—it's been a hell of a long time.'

She nodded and came in, perching on the edge

of the chair opposite him and eyeing him warily. 'I'm not really being fair to you, am I? You're not used to this, and you must be bored to death.'

'I am. There's just nothing for me to do except think about you and wonder what the hell I did that was so wrong.'

'Nothing. You did nothing. That was the trouble, Max. You just carried on as you always had, and took me with you. And it wasn't enough.'

'It was enough for me. I loved working with you—watching your incredible ability to organise and sort stuff. Things just happened when you were around, and it was amazing. I didn't realise what I'd got until I lost you.'

She sighed softly, and huddled further down in her dressing gown. 'Max, if this is going to work, you're going to have to cut back on your time in the office, you know that, don't you? Your time away, particularly. It's just not conducive to family life.'

'My family managed. My father worked the same sort of hours.'

'And he died of a heart attack at forty-nine! That's only eleven years away for you, Max. Your daughters will be just starting secondary school. And I'll be a widow at forty-four. That's not something to look forward to.'

God. Eleven years? Was that all? No wonder his mother had found another man to share her life. She was only sixty-two now, fit and active and full of life. And her husband had died far too young; he could see that now.

Was that in store for him? Would he go to work one day and find not his PA but the Grim Reaper waiting for him, as his father had?

'I'm doing it for us,' he said, but his words had a hollow ring to them, and she shook her head.

'No. You're doing it for you, because you can, because you're driven by the need to succeed, but there are other ways to succeed, Max—other things you can do.'

'Such as?'

She shrugged. 'Be a good father to your children? Enjoy your life? Take up a hobby— sport of some kind. Not running. That's just a solitary thing you do to stop you thinking.'

Hell. Was there anything this woman missed?

'Fancy a game of chess?' she asked out of the blue, and he stared at her and then gave a soft chuckle.

'Yeah, why not? Although I'll probably beat you.'

'I doubt it. I've been practising. I play with John when he's here.'

Him again.

'Does he beat you?'

'Not often.'

Well, there was a challenge. He leant back and smiled. 'Bring it on,' he said softly.

Oh, dear. She recognised that look.

Oh, well, at least it wouldn't be boring. She got the chess pieces out, opened the coffee-table to reveal a chess board, then took a black and a white pawn, shuffled them behind her back and held her closed fists out.

'Right,' he said, and she opened her right hand and sighed at his smug grin.

'OK, you start,' she said, and handed him the white pieces.

It was all downhill from there, really, because she was finding it really hard to concentrate.

'Check.'

She stared at the board in disbelief. What on earth had happened to her? She'd completely lost her focus.

She moved her queen, he tutted and took her bishop, and said, 'Check.'

Again? She stared at the board for ages, con-scious of Max's hands dangling loosely between his knees, his shoulders hunched over, broad and square and powerful, his head so close she could see the individual hairs, soft and glossy and so enticing.

'Are you sure you want to do that?'

She looked down at the board, muttered under her breath and changed her mind, then sat back. 'OK.'

'Oh, dear.' He moved his final piece, gave her a wicked smile and murmured, 'I believe you'll find that's checkmate.'

What? 'Oh, rats,' she said, slumping back against the chair. 'I'd forgotten how good you are.'

'I'll take that as a compliment,' he said with a smile, and set the pieces up again.

'Oh, no,' she said, laughing and holding up her hands. 'Not tonight. I'm tired and I'm just not focusing. We'll have another go tomorrow.'

By which time she'd have pulled herself together and repossessed her mind.

'Right, it really is time for bed,' she said, and met his eyes. 'Max, why don't you have an early night?'

'What, and lie just feet away from you and think about you? I don't think so. It's been over a year, Jules. That's a long time.'

And then it occurred to her that, in that year,

there might have been another woman. Several, in fact. Did she want to know?

Yes.

'Have you—have there…?' She trailed off, unable to say the words, but he understood and let his breath out on a huff of disbelief.

'You really think that of me? Julia, we're married. I may not have been the best husband, but I meant my vows. I haven't looked at, or touched, or thought about another woman since I met you. And, since you left me, I've thought about very little else. So, forgive me if I don't want to go upstairs and lie down politely within spitting distance of you and go quietly to sleep!'

She felt hot colour scorch her cheeks, and stood up hastily and headed for the door. 'I'm sorry. I didn't mean to be so insensitive. For what it's worth, I've missed you, too.'

'Jules! Julia, wait!'

She stopped, her hand on the latch, and he came up behind her and turned her gently into his arms.

'I'm sorry. I'm just ratty because I need you. I'm feeling like a caged lion at the moment, and I'm lashing out at anything in range. And it just happens to be you, every time. And it's rubbish, because all I want to do is hold you—'

And, without another word, he folded her

carefully against his chest and rested his head against hers. She could feel his heart beating, feel the tension radiating off him, but she knew it would go no further, that he wouldn't kiss her or touch her or do anything she didn't invite directly, because for all his faults he loved her.

'Oh, Max,' she sighed, and, sliding her arms around him, she held him close. 'I'm sorry it's so difficult.'

'It doesn't need to be. You could come back to me.'

'We've been through that,' she reminded him, and eased out of his arms. 'I'm not coming back—not until I have concrete proof that you're changing for good. And, so far, there's no evidence of that at all.'

He stared down at her sombrely, then nodded. 'OK. So tomorrow, let's go to London, and we'll go to the office and I'll make some calls and see what I can do. And I'd like to go and see my mother.'

His mother! Of course! She'd missed her. Linda Gallagher was the closest thing she had to a mother now, and she knew the woman would be more than supportive of her in trying to get Max to cut back on his hours. After all, she'd lost her own husband far too young, and she wouldn't want the same thing to happen to her son. And she'd adore the babies.

'Have you told her yet?'

He shook his head. 'No. How can I? I don't have a phone,' he said with irony, and she sighed.

'You could have used the house phone for that.'

'Only I don't have the number.'

'You should know your mother's number,' she chided, and he shrugged.

'Why? It's in my phone—only, silly me, I don't have my phone any more, it seems, because it's been confiscated.'

'I'd give it back to you if I felt I could trust you,' she said frankly, and his mouth twitched.

'Better keep it, then,' he said softly, and, bending his head, he brushed his lips over hers. 'Go to bed, Jules. I'll see you in the morning— and we'll go and sort everything out.'

If only she could believe it.

CHAPTER SIX

'I'D BETTER make some calls,' he said as they sat over breakfast the next morning. 'Prime Andrea.'

'What about your mother?'

He pulled a face. 'Yeah. Her, too. But mostly business.'

'I'll get your phone,' she said, and ran upstairs to retrieve it from the safety of her bedroom. She went back down and handed it to him. 'You seem to have a few missed calls that have got under Andrea's radar,' she said wryly, and he glanced at the screen and gave a frustrated sigh.

'I have to deal with some of these.'

'I don't doubt it. You've got an hour,' she told him, and, scooping up the babies, she took them upstairs and bathed and dressed them.

'You're going to meet your grandmother today,' she told them with a smile. 'She's going to love you.' But she might not be so warm with her daughter-in-law, Julia realised sadly, her smile fading. A whole year—more—of being out of contact while Max had searched for her might not have done anything to endear her to the woman, and she regretted that.

But how could she have stayed in touch and yet not have kept Max informed? She couldn't, but she felt another stab of guilt. Max might not have been the most reasonable of husbands, but he'd never kept anything from her, and she was beginning to realise just how much she'd done him wrong by not telling him she was pregnant.

'Oh, Ava, no!' she cried, reaching out and catching the baby before she toppled over backwards. 'When did you learn to stand up? You're going to be such a pixie, aren't you?'

Ava grinned and giggled, and, grabbing hold of the edge of the quilt in her fat little fists, she pulled herself up again.

'You're trouble,' she said, and then realised Libby was crawling out of the door and heading for the top of the stairs. 'Libby!' she called, and ran after her, to find Max sitting on the top step with his daughter in his arms, rubbing noses and laughing.

'I think you need a stairgate,' he said, and she nodded.

'I do. I bought one, but I can't fit it. It's not wide enough. I've been meaning to find another one.'

'I'll sort it,' he said, and, getting to his feet, he hoisted Libby up in the air and blew a raspberry on her tummy.

Heavens. Max, blowing raspberries? Maybe there was hope after all…

Andrea was amazing.

Crisp, efficient, much too old for Max—in case she'd been worried—and about as approachable as a pet piranha, but she took one look at them both that morning and smiled. 'Good,' she said to Max. 'You're looking like a human being at last. You needed a break.'

'I'm going crazy,' he said bluntly, but Andrea just smiled at him and then switched her attention to Julia.

'So—is he behaving?'

Julia rolled her eyes. 'Sort of. He keeps trying to steal his phone from me.'

'Well, he will. He plays hardball, you should know that.'

'But it's not a game.'

'No. I think he realises. If he didn't, he wouldn't be there with you. Now, if I might borrow him for a little while, there are several urgent things he needs to deal with and then you can have him back.'

'You can come,' he said to her. 'See what we're up to.'

And be sucked in? 'We'll be fine,' she said, deciding to trust him, and she settled on a chair in her old office with the babies at her feet and looked around.

Odd, how alien it seemed, and yet how familiar. Nothing had really changed, only her—and she'd changed beyond recognition, apparently, if the blank look on the face of the man who stuck his head round the door was anything to go by.

'Oh—sorry. I was looking for Andrea,' he said.

She smiled at the familiar face. 'Hello, Stephen,' she said, and he did a mild double-take and stared at her.

'Julia?'

'That's me,' she said lightly, wondering whether to be flattered or not, and Stephen gave a startled laugh.

'Well—how are you? I thought—' He broke off, clearly unsure quite what to say, and for the first time she wondered about the public rather than private impact that her disappearance had had on Max.

'I've been busy,' she said wryly, and he stared at the girls and gave a tiny, choked laugh.

'I can see. Amazing. I had no idea.'

Nor had Max, but she wasn't going to discuss their private life with one of his employees, even if he had once been a friend of hers, and one of Max's most reliable right-hand men.

The most reliable. 'So how's Yashimoto?'

'Stunned. You know Max is selling the company back to him?'

It was her turn to stare. 'He is?'

'Yes, apparently. I couldn't believe it. He's fought so hard to turn it round, and now he's just giving it away. Still, it's in much better shape, and Yashimoto will make a better job of it now with the benefit of Max's advice, so he's happy. But it's Max I can't fathom. I thought you would have known all about it, since you were so involved with setting up the deal in the first place.'

She shook her head. 'Max and I don't talk about business now.'

'No. Good idea, not taking work home. Doesn't sound like Max, but babies change you. Did you know we've had a little boy?'

She smiled. 'No, I didn't. Congratulations— and make sure you see plenty of him.'

'I will. In the meantime, I'd better go and join this meeting.'

'I think they're in Max's office.'

'Cheers. And it's lovely to see you again.'

He shut the door and left her there to contemplate the bombshell he'd dropped.

When had Max decided to sell Yashimoto's company back to him? Yesterday? Today? Or much earlier, and she just hadn't known because they hadn't discussed business at all, as she'd told Stephen?

She had no idea, but she was puzzled, whatever. Did it mean he was taking her seriously and cutting back on his business interests? Or had it already been in the pipeline? She needed to know, because the difference was crucial. She didn't want to go thinking that he was making sweeping changes when all the time he'd been following one of his incredible hunches.

Oh, well. She'd find out later. In the meantime, she had bigger things to worry about, because shortly she was going to see her mother-in-law again, and she was feeling curiously apprehensive.

She needn't have worried.

Linda Gallagher took one look at her with the

girls, clapped a hand over her mouth and burst into tears.

'Oh, Julia, my dear girl—oh, my dear, dear, girl!' And, without another word, she threw her arms around her and hugged her hard.

Julia blinked away her own tears and hugged her back, and then she was released, and Linda was exclaiming over the babies and crying on Max and hugging him until she thought his ribs would break.

'Come in—come on in, all of you. Richard? Look, it's Max, and he's brought Julia and—'

And she started to cry again.

'Julia?'

Richard, Linda's partner, studied her for a moment and then gave a fleeting smile and kissed her cheek. 'It's good to see you again. And you've been busy.'

'A little,' she said wryly. 'I'm sorry to drop such a bombshell on you. It seems to be a day for them.'

Because Max *had* only decided to sell back to Yashimoto this morning, she'd found out. So he was taking her seriously, and going to huge lengths to change things.

Max took charge of the babies, tucking one under each arm and heading into the house with his mother fussing, clucking and mopping up her tears, and Richard helped her take the seats out of the car and into the house so the girls could sit in them to have their lunch.

'I'm so glad you're here,' he said quietly as he closed the front door. 'Linda's really missed you, and Max has been—well—difficult doesn't even scratch the surface.'

She shook her head. 'I'm sorry.'

'No. Don't worry about me. But Linda probably deserves an explanation, when you can give her one, and—it's between you and Max, really, I guess. But it's great to see you again, and to see him smiling. And a father. That's not something we thought we'd ever see.'

'No. None of us thought that.'

Well, not as long as he was with her, at least, what with her medical problems. But apparently miracles did happen, and she had two of them.

Three, if Max turning his life around was to be believed. She still wasn't sure he was, but time would tell.

In the meantime, she followed Richard into the sitting room and found Linda on the floor with her back to the sofa, and Libby crawling busily over her while Ava headed for the plant stand in the corner.

'I don't think so,' she said, disengaging her fingers from the fine mahogany legs of the stand before she pulled it over on herself. 'You need to be put in the stocks, young lady. Come and say hello to your grandmother.'

And, turning her round, she dangled her across the room by her fingers, while her little legs tried valiantly to keep up.

'She's going to walk early,' Linda said, shaking her head. 'Just like Max. He was a nightmare. And she won't be far behind,' she added, grabbing Libby, who was climbing up her front and trying to get on the sofa. 'How on earth do you keep up with them?'

She gave a tired laugh. 'Oh, I have no idea. It's getting worse by the day. I thought when they were in ITU and I'd just had my C-section that it couldn't get any worse—'

'You had a C-section?'

Max's face was shocked, and she realised she hadn't actually told him anything about their birth.

'Yes,' she said softly. 'I had to. The adhesions were too bad, they wouldn't contemplate letting me deliver, especially not at thirty-three weeks.'

His face was ashen. She had no idea why the idea had shocked him so much, but obviously it had, and she realised she'd done yet another thing wrong. *Oh, Max.*

'Hey, it's OK, we're all fine,' she assured him, but he still looked pale.

'You should have called me,' Linda said gently. 'I would have come and helped you.'

'And told Max?'

Her face contorted, and she swallowed hard and bit her lip. 'I'm sorry; it's none of my business.'

'It's not you,' she said hurriedly. 'We were just having problems—'

'*You* were having problems. I was too wrapped up in my life to realise,' he said, his fairness and honesty amazing her yet again. 'Julia pointed out to me yesterday that I'm only eleven years younger than Dad was when he died. And I don't want to go the same way.'

'Good,' Linda said, her eyes filling. 'He was a good man, your father, but he didn't know when to stop, and I've been so worried about you. Maybe this was exactly what you needed to bring you to your senses.'

'Well, let's hope so,' Julia said quietly. 'Linda, I could do with heating some food for them. They're going to start to yell in a minute; they've had a long morning.'

'Of course. Come on through to the kitchen; the men can look after them for a minute.'

And, Julia thought realistically, it would give Linda a chance to grill her about her motives.

Except she didn't, not at first; she just put the kettle on, put the baby food in the microwave and then turned and gave Julia a hug.

'Oh, I've missed you,' she said, letting her go. 'I realise you couldn't contact me if you felt you couldn't talk to Max, but I have missed you.'

'I've missed you, too,' she said with a lump in her throat. 'I could have done with a mum while they were in hospital. I had Jane, but she'd just had her own baby, and it was difficult for her.'

Linda's face was troubled, and after a moment she said, 'Do you mind if I ask you something? Why didn't you tell him you were pregnant? Was it because of Debbie?'

'Debbie?' she asked, a feeling of foreboding washing over her. 'Who's Debbie?'

Linda's face was a mass of conflicting emotions. 'He hasn't told you?' she said in the end, and Julia shook her head.

'I know nothing about anyone called Debbie. Who is she? Don't tell me he's having an affair—'

'No! Oh, good grief, no, nothing like that. Oh, my goodness—' She covered her mouth with her hand and stared at Julia, then shook her head and flapped her hand as if she was seeking a way out. 'Um—I'm sorry, I shouldn't have said anything. It's not my story to tell. You'll have to ask Max. Oh, dear God, I can't believe he hasn't told you.'

'Is it something to do with why he doesn't want children?' she asked, watching Linda carefully, but Linda obviously felt she'd said more than enough, and she shook her head and held up her hand.

'No. I'm sorry, darling, I can't tell you. You'll have to talk to Max, but—tread carefully. At the time— No, you'll have to ask him yourself, I can't say any more.' She straightened up, the pots of food in her hand, and found a smile. 'Come on, let's go and feed the babies. I never thought I'd ever be a grandmother, and I don't intend to waste a minute of it.'

They had a lovely afternoon.

After lunch—which his mother had thrown together after a hasty trip to the supermarket deli-counter earlier when he'd phoned to warn her they were coming—they took the babies out for a walk on Hampstead Heath.

'We should have brought Murphy,' he said, but Julia just laughed.

'I don't think so. He's better off at home. He'd be a nightmare in the mud, and your mother's house isn't exactly designed for dogs, with all that pale carpet.'

'OK,' he said with a wry grin. 'Maybe you're right.'

'Of course I'm right. I'm—' She broke off, and he eyed her thoughtfully.

'Always right?' he offered, and she shook her head, tears she'd scarcely shed before this week filling her eyes for the hundredth time.

'I'm sorry.'

'Hey, not now. We're having a happy day.'

He held out his hand, and after a moment she slipped her fingers into his and squeezed, but there was a bit of her that wondered if he was putting on a show for his mother's benefit.

But he didn't hold her hand for long, because the buggy got stuck and he had to go and help Richard lift it up some steps, and then his mother put her arm through his and started to talk to him, and Julia was left with Richard and the babies.

'He's looking better.'

'He needed to. He was haggard when he

arrived on Monday. I was shocked. I'd managed to convince myself that he didn't care—'

'Didn't care?' Richard gave a short cough of laughter. 'Oh, no. He cared. I've never seen a man so tortured. He was devastated when he couldn't find you. I really think he imagined you were dead.'

Oh, lord. She closed her eyes for a second and stumbled, but Richard caught her arm and gave it a reassuring squeeze.

'You'll sort it out between you,' he said comfortingly. 'Just give it time.'

She'd given it two weeks, and nearly a third of that was gone. It was Thursday now, and he'd been there since Monday. So that was another ten days. Would it be enough to convince her that he'd changed? Or enough for him to know just what he was taking on?

She didn't know. But Yashimoto was going to be out of the picture soon, and that meant no more trips to Tokyo. If he could do the same with the New York operation, so he only had his UK businesses to worry about, then maybe, just maybe, they'd be all right.

But, in the meantime, she had to find a way of asking him about Debbie, and, until she knew exactly who she was and what she meant to him, she had no idea what the future might hold. She just knew that, if Linda was to be believed, Debbie was hugely significant.

If only she knew what it was she was asking him…

'Poor old Murphs. Did we abandon you, mate?'

Max ruffled his ears and stroked his side, and Murphy leant against him and thumped his tail enthusiastically.

'I think that means "feed me",' Jules said drily, and he laughed and picked up his bowl.

'Hungry, are you?' he said, and the tail went faster. 'Shall I feed him?'

'Mmm—but, if you could take him out for a run first, that would be great. I'll bath the girls.'

'Are you sure you can manage?'

'I'm fine. Go on, off you go.'

So he took him out for a run by the river, just for a few minutes, because the light was fading fast, and by the time they got home it was gloomy and Julia was in the kitchen with the girls giving them their supper and their evening feed.

'Tea?' he offered, knowing now that she liked to drink while she was feeding, and she smiled her thanks and settled down on the sofa with the babies.

He put her tea—with cold water—in reach, and sat down with his at the other end of the table and watched her feeding them while Murphy chased his bowl around the tiled floor.

'I might buy him a bowl with a rubber base,' she said ruefully, and Max laughed and sipped his tea and watched his wife and daughters, and thought that life had never been more complex or more challenging—or more fulfilling.

Happy families, he thought, and wondered how long it would last. He'd done his best—handed Yashimoto the deal of the century—but he didn't care and it made him feel good, because the man had worked hard to turn his old company around, and, given a leg up, he'd be fine now.

But that was just the tip of the iceberg, of course. There was a ton of other investments which still needed his serious intervention, and with his eye off the ball— Well, who knew what could happen to it? He'd had to rescue a situation this morning because he hadn't been on hand to deal with it, and Stephen had been tied up with Tokyo.

And for some reason Andrea hadn't flagged it up to him.

Oh, well. It was sorted now, but he wasn't

sure how much longer he could pretend his empire could run itself.

'Are you hungry?' he asked her, watching as she detached Libby and sat her up.

'Starving. Why? What did you have in mind?'

He chuckled. 'Nothing with garlic. I was wondering if I should get something from the pub again.'

'Oh. That would be lovely. They do a really great thing with mozzarella and basil, a little tartlet. It's fabulous. And sticky-toffee pudding.'

'Stick— That sounds gross,' he said with a laugh.

'No. It's gorgeous. You ought to try it.'

'I'll try some of yours.'

'If I let you have any.'

'Oh, you will,' he said, taking Ava off her and wincing at the deafening burp. 'I'll sweet-talk you.'

'You can try,' she said, but her eyes were twinkling and he felt a sudden stab of longing. Damn. After the conversation they'd had last night, there was no way he was getting that close to her, so he'd be better off not thinking about it.

'Come on, pest. Let's take you up and change your nappy and tuck you up in bed, so your mother and father can have a little civilised conversation.'

'Better keep them here, then,' Jules said from behind him, and he turned back and caught her teasing smile, and felt desire lance through him again, hot and hard and needy.

It was going to be a long, long evening.

She lit the fire while he was over at the pub collecting their order, and by the time he came back the logs were blazing merrily behind the fireguard and the table was laid.

'Is that woodsmoke I can smell?' he asked, coming back into the kitchen, and she nodded.

'I've lit the fire. I thought maybe we could play chess again, or watch some of the baby DVDs.'

She saw his smile slip. 'OK. That would be nice,' he said, and made a valiant attempt to resurrect the smile, but it didn't fool her. And the first time they'd watched a DVD of the babies it had upset him. But why?

'Max?'

'Fancy a small glass of wine? There's a bit of white left, or I've bought some rosé.'

'Oh. Rosé would be nice. Thanks,' she said, and let it drop for now.

* * *

She was watching him.

He ignored her, handing her the stacked plates with their covers and swiftly twisting the cork out of the wine. By the time he'd poured it and sat down opposite her, she was busy concentrating on her food, and, with the smell of the sticky-toffee pudding drifting from its resting place on the side of the Aga, he thought he might have got away with it.

For now. But the DVD's were a minefield, making him feel raw, and he wasn't sure he could watch a film shot in special care. Not see how close they'd come—

'Wow, that was gorgeous. Thanks, Max.'

He put aside his black thoughts and smiled at her. She looked lovely tonight, her hair loose around her shoulders and her eyes warm and gentle. If only…

No. Not yet. She'd said so, with knobs on, but, if he could only get that close to her, maybe he could convince her to come back to him.

'It's a pleasure,' he said. 'So—how about letting me thrash you at chess again?'

She hesitated for a second, then gave him a mischievous grin. 'OK. If you don't mind being beaten. I've remembered how your mind works.'

'Faster than yours,' he pointed out, and she stuck her tongue out at him and stood up.

'Let's see, shall we?'

'Indeed. Best of three?'

'You think it'll take that many?'

'No. Two will be more than enough to have you whimpering off with your tail between your legs,' he retorted, following her with the dog in his wake.

That was a mistake, because he almost had her for the second time when Murphy stood up and walked round the table, and, seizing her chance, Julia called him all excitedly, and his tail thrashed and cleared the board.

'Oh, dear, what a shame, we'll have to start again,' she said with a wicked grin, but he wasn't having it.

'I can remember where every piece was,' he said, and proceeded to reset the chessmen in place.

'Your knight wasn't there.'

'Yes it was.'

'No. It was there. Your bishop was there.'

'Rubbish. How could my bishop have got there? Let's face it, Jules, I've thrashed you,' he said, lounging back on the sofa and crossing his ankle over the other knee. 'Just admit it.'

'Never.'

'I never had you down as a cheat,' he said softly, and she stopped in her tracks and stared at him.

'I wasn't cheating! I was just teasing, Max. Trying to lighten the atmosphere.'

He swallowed. 'What's wrong with the atmosphere?'

'I don't know, but ever since I mentioned the DVDs you've been funny. Why don't you want to see them?'

'I do,' he lied. Well, it wasn't really a lie, but he was scared and sick inside, and emotions he'd buried too long ago were bubbling to the surface. And he didn't want to deal with them.

She got up and cleared away the chess pieces, folded the lid of the coffee-table over and straightened it, then dimmed the lights and switched on the television. 'OK, then,' she said quietly. 'This is the next one—the babies in hospital. We were about to watch it the other night when you walked out.'

'Just put it on, Jules,' he said gruffly, his left hand wrapped tightly round the stem of the wine glass, and, before he knew what she was going to do, she'd started the disc and had taken hold of his right hand, wrapping it in both of hers and snuggling up against his shoulder.

'OK, that's Ava. She was stronger. She was born first, and, although she was smaller, she was better developed and she's heavier now than Libby. And that's Libby. She had to have much more help with her breathing, and there were a few days when—when we thought we might lose her,' she said a little unsteadily, and he realised she was struggling just as much as he was. Her fingers tightened on his, and he squeezed them back, as much for himself as for her.

'They look tiny.'

'They were. Twins are always smaller. They've only got half as much room, so considering that they do pretty well, but by the time they were delivered my uterus had reached its limit and it was in danger of rupturing. They had to do two operations to free the adhesions, and then finally they couldn't release any more and they had to deliver them. But I hung on as long as I could.'

'It sounds awful,' he said, wincing at the thought. It must have been so painful. Why on earth hadn't she contacted him? Although God alone knows what use he would have been to her, haunted by his demons.

'It was. And I was so scared. I nearly called you. If you'd rung before, I would have done, but then my phone was stolen and all I could do was get by, minute by minute, and then the crisis was over.'

'I would have come,' he said gruffly.

'Would you?'

She turned and looked at him, and he met her gentle, searching eyes briefly before he turned away. 'Yes,' he said with conviction. 'I would.' Even though it would have killed him.

'Max, can I ask you something?'

He looked back at her, and his heart started to pound. 'Sure.'

'Who's Debbie?'

The wine sloshed over the rim of the glass, soaking his hand and running over the arm of the sofa. He leapt to his feet and got a cloth, dabbing and blotting and rubbing with it until she took it out of his hand and pulled him back down gently onto the sofa beside her.

'Max, forget that, talk to me. Who is she? Why was your mother so surprised that I'd never heard of her? And what did she do to you that's made you so shut down inside?'

He stared at her, his breath rasping, then he closed his mouth and swallowed. He could do this. He owed it to her—and he should have told her years ago.

'She was my girlfriend,' he said, his voice sounding strange to his ears. Rough and unused. Like his feelings. 'She was pregnant, and she got pre-eclampsia. They did a C-section, but she was fitting when they took her into Theatre, and she died. So did the baby. My son. He lived for fifteen hours and seven minutes. He was twenty-six weeks. That's why the DVD—'

He clenched his jaw, holding back the tears, keeping it all under control. For an age she said nothing, but then she dragged in a shaky breath and said, 'Did he have a name? Your baby?'

'Ye—' He swallowed and tried again. 'Yes. I called him Michael. It was my father's name.'

'Oh, Max.'

The tears welled in her eyes and splashed down over her cheeks, and she covered her mouth with her hand and tried to hold in the sob.

He couldn't look at her. Couldn't watch her crying for Debbie and their tiny son, or for him, so locked in grief that he couldn't even watch a film of his own daughters without replaying his baby's short, desperate hours. He couldn't watch it, or her, because, if he did, if he let the feelings up to the surface, they'd tear him apart like they had before, and he couldn't take it all over again.

'Oh, Max,' she murmured, and he felt her fingers stroke away the tears that he could feel running soundlessly down his cheeks.

'It's OK, Max, I've got you,' she said gently, and he realised that, far from tearing him apart, it felt good to let it go, because Jules was with him, and he wasn't alone any more.

And so with a quiet sigh he turned into her arms, and for the first time in fifteen years he let the tears flow unchecked.

CHAPTER SEVEN

HE SLEPT until nine the following morning, the only time she'd ever known him to sleep late.

Even jet-lagged, he'd never slept for so long, so she crept into his room at eight to check that he was still breathing and found him lying spreadeagled on his front across the bed, snoring softly. The covers had slipped off one side, but the room was warm, so even though he was naked he wouldn't be cold.

The urge to pull the covers up over him and creep in beside him and take him in her arms almost overwhelmed her, but instead she tiptoed out and went back downstairs and put the washing on, then let Murphy out into the garden for a romp. He brought her his ball on a rope, and she threw it for him a few times, but it was chilly out, and she didn't like to leave the girls. They were getting so adventurous, and even in the playpen she didn't trust them not to get up to mischief.

So she went back inside, and she put the radio on quietly and folded the washing that had aired overnight on the front of the Aga and made herself a coffee. Then, just when she was convincing herself he hadn't been breathing at all and she'd imagined it, she heard the boards creak and the water running in the bathroom, and she gave a sigh of relief and relaxed.

They'd talked for hours last night. He'd told her all about it; about how he'd met Debbie, and how excited they'd been when they'd found out she was pregnant. And he talked about little Michael, and how he'd held him as he died, and how he'd vowed then never to put another woman at such risk.

'So it wasn't that you didn't want children?' she'd asked, pushing him, and he'd shaken his head emphatically.

'Oh, no. I would have loved children, and the girls— Well, they're just amazing. The most precious gift imaginable. I just can't believe we've got them. But I don't know if I could have coped with the pregnancy.'

'So what would you have done if I'd told you?' she'd asked, and he'd shrugged.

'I don't know. I don't know if I could have gone through all those weeks of waiting, knowing it wasn't going to be straightforward, watching you suffer, waiting for something awful to happen. I think it would have torn me apart.'

'And if we were to have another?'

His eyes had been tortured. 'I don't know if I could take it. I'd rather not find out. We've been so lucky to have the girls. Let's not push it.'

Not that it was really an issue. She didn't really want to get pregnant again after the last time, and the doctors hadn't seemed to think it would be a good idea, but in any case, until their relationship was a great deal more secure, there was no way she was going to risk it.

Even assuming she let him get that close.

But one thing she knew. She wasn't going to let him sweep it all back under the carpet again. She was going to make him talk about it—about Debbie, and the baby, and how he felt about it— if it killed him. He owed it to them not to let them be forgotten, and so their memory would be treasured, and kept alive, and their girls would know one day that, a long time ago, they'd had a brother.

Oh, hell.

She scrubbed the tears from her eyes and looked up as he walked in, and he took one look at her and sighed gently.

'Oh, Jules. Are you OK?'

'Sorry. I was just thinking about when we tell the girls, when they're older.'

He gave a strangled laugh. 'Talk about crossing bridges before you get to them. Anyway, never mind that. What does a man have to do round here to get a cup of tea?'

'Put the kettle on?' she suggested, and he put it on the hob and crouched down and said hello to the babies, who sat happily in the playpen chewing on blocks.

'I think they're teething,' he said in wonder, and she laughed and got up.

'Of course they're teething. They'll do little else for the next umpteen weeks. Apart from try and escape from whatever means of restraint we put them in.'

'We'll have to try handcuffs,' he said, and she put her hand over his mouth.

'Shh,' she said. 'Not in front of the children.'

And he laughed, the first real, proper laugh she'd heard from him in years, and then the laughter faded and their eyes locked, and he stopped breathing.

She knew that, because she could see his chest freeze, and his heart was pounding, the pulse visible in the hollow of his throat, beating in time with hers. And then he seemed to come out of the trance and dragged in a breath and looked away. Somehow that freed her, too, so she made tea and put bread in the mesh toast-holder that went under the cover of the hotplate, and when the water was boiling she made a pot of tea and put the wire holder under the cover to toast the bread—and all the time all she could think about was the sound of his laugh, and how the tears last night seemed to have freed his emotions.

Did that mean he'd be able to play?

She hoped so. She'd always known there was another side of him, one he kept shut down, and she couldn't wait to meet the other Max.

'So what are we going to do today?' she asked.

'What's it like outside?'

'Cold. Bright and sunny, but cold. The wind's chilly.'

'So—something indoors? How about going to find a better stairgate?'

'That's a good idea. And they could do with some more clothes, if we're going to one of the big shops. They're growing like weeds.'

'That'll be chewing the loo brush,' he said drily, and she stared at him in horror.

'What?'

'Ava,' he told her, and she looked down at her

elder daughter in the playpen, happily gumming away on a plastic toy, and felt sick.

'When?'

'The other day in the bathroom. Don't worry, she didn't actually get it in her mouth,' he said, and she realised he'd been joking and felt her shoulders sag.

'Is that how it ended up on the window sill?'

'Yup.'

'Oh, the little horror. She's never done that before.'

'Probably because you're more efficient with them than I am. She was at a loose end for rather too long while I prevaricated about the temperature of the water. So—shopping?'

She stared at him. He sounded—good grief—almost enthusiastic. He'd *never* sounded enthusiastic about shopping before. He'd hardly ever *gone* shopping before. Except for clothes, and that was more a case of visiting his tailor for suits and shirts. She'd always bought anything less critical for him, and always in a stolen moment from the office during a meeting that he was attending without her.

Quite simply, there had never been *time* for shopping in their old life, and, if he was looking forward to it now, well, she wasn't going to waste the experience.

'Let's go to Lakeside,' she suggested. 'There are all sorts of shops there, and it's all under cover, so we don't have to worry about the babies getting cold. We can make a day of it.'

She hadn't been joking.

He hadn't really believed that there could be so many shops all selling similar things lined up row after row after row. Well, he'd known they existed, of course he did, but that they should be so heaving with people on a February weekday stunned him.

But they found a stairgate for the babies, and lots of clothes, nappies and toys—so many, in fact, that he ended up making more than one trip back to the car to offload them. And there was a special baby zone, where they were able to feed and change the babies, and for once he managed not to get too messy.

Then it was back to the fray, and he caught Jules looking longingly at a clothes shop. For women.

'When did you last buy anything new?' he asked, and she smiled wryly.

'What, apart from jeans and jumpers? I can't remember. But I don't need anything else.'

'Yes, you do,' he told her. 'Of course you do.'

'When for?'

He shrugged. 'When I take you out for dinner?'

'What, with the babies in tow?'

'No. When we get a babysitter.'

'I don't know a babysitter—well, apart from Jane, and she won't want to babysit for me in the evening. I usually take the girls round to her if I need to go somewhere where I can't take them.'

'My mother?'

'Linda? She lives in London.'

'She'd come up.'

'What—just so you can take me out for dinner? That's a bit of an ask.'

'We could stay there.'

In their old room? The one where they'd stayed in the past? She was looking doubtful, and he realised why.

'Sorry. I'm getting ahead of the game here, but—why not buy a dress? Something pretty. A top, maybe, if you don't want a dress, or some new trousers. You can always dress up at home, if you want to.'

'But I don't,' she said bluntly, and he blinked.

She was looking at him as if he'd suggested something wrong, and it dawned on him that she was taking it as a criticism of her clothes.

'Oh, Jules, don't get uppity. I wasn't criticising. I just thought—if you wanted something pretty—' He broke off. 'It doesn't matter. Forget it. I'm sorry.'

And, without waiting for her response, he walked away.

Damn.

Had she misread him? Because she'd *love* to buy some new clothes, something pretty that fitted her new, different body and made her feel like a woman again instead of a milk machine.

Underwear. Pretty, sexy underwear.

For Max?

Maybe. God knows he wasn't seeing her in her nursing bras.

And a pretty top, and some nice, well-cut trousers that didn't cling to her lumpy thighs like glue. None of her old trousers fitted her any more. They were all too tight, but she'd been stick-thin when they'd been jetting all over the place, because there had quite simply never been time to eat.

But she had time now, and the inclination, to keep herself well, and so she had curves where she'd never had curves before.

She grabbed the hands of the baby buggy and ran after him. 'Max? Max, stop! Please!'

He stopped, and she caught up with him and tried a smile. 'I'm sorry. I misunderstood—and you're right. I'd love to get some new things. I actually *need* to get some new things. Can you bear it?'

'Only if I get to see them as you try them on.'

'Oh. I was talking about underwear, really.'

His eyes flared, then darkened. 'Even better,' he murmured, and she felt a soft tide of colour sweep over her cheeks.

'You can't—'

'Maybe not in the shop,' he agreed. 'But later.'

She swallowed. 'OK, forget the underwear,' she said hastily, and he pulled a face, but he laughed anyway.

'So, what else?'

'Just—tops, trousers. It won't take long.'

He snorted. 'I'm not that naïve. Why don't I take the kids with me and leave you to it for an hour or so? You can ring me when you're ready, and I'll come and pay.'

'You don't have to pay!' she protested, but he just raised an eyebrow.

'Jules, you're my *wife*,' he said firmly. 'And

I will quite happily pay for your clothes. I've just paid several hundred thousand pounds for the sake of spending a little time with you. I don't think the odd top or pair of trousers is going to make a whole lot of difference.'

Oh, lord. She'd thought the Yashimoto deal was a bit hasty. Now she was beginning to realise just how much he'd invested in their relationship, and she looked at him with new eyes.

'I'm sorry. I didn't mean for you to do that.'

'Jules, it's fine. I'm happy with it. It was a good decision. And we're talking about a cut in profits, more than a deficit, so forget it. Now, my phone?'

'Oh. Yes.' She rummaged in her bag and found his phone, but, as she handed it over, there was a bit of her that wondered if he'd suggested this as a way of getting the phone off her.

'No. Trust me.'

Had she said it out loud? 'Sorry. Right, I'll be as quick as I can. Don't leave them.'

He gave her a look, then turned away and headed off into the crowd, leaving her feeling suddenly empty-handed and at a loss.

Come on, Julia, she told herself. Organisation. Underwear first, then a top, then trousers.

And she headed into a large top-end department store, found the lingerie and started shopping.

'How long can she take, girls?' he asked, crouching down in front of the now-restless babies and trying to entertain them. 'She said she wouldn't be long.'

He gave a rueful little laugh, and Ava reached out her hand and gurgled at him. 'Da-da,' she said, and he felt his eyes fill.

'Oh, you clever little girl,' he said, struggling not to embarrass himself in public, but then she said, 'Mama,' and he realised she was just babbling.

Idiot him. Of course she was.

He straightened up and looked around. What could he do to entertain them? There was a book shop, so he headed in there, all ready to find books for them to suck and chew and hurl on the floor, but then he saw cookery books.

Books for idiots. Books for people who'd never lifted a spatula in their lives. People like him.

He'd cook for her. He'd find a book that seemed straightforward and comprehensive, he'd find a recipe, and they'd drop into the supermarket on the way home and he'd cook for her.

Fish. She loved fish. Fresh tuna? He thumbed through the recipe books, found one that looked promising, checked out tuna and discovered that it took seconds. Whap-whap on a hot griddle and it was done. Excellent. And he could serve it with salad and new potatoes. Even he couldn't screw those up.

He bought the book, hung the bag on the back of the buggy and then reached for his phone.

She was engaged. Damn. Oh, well, he'd give her a minute. She might be trying to call him. He was about to slip it back into his pocket when it rang, and he answered it instantly.

'You were on the phone!' she said accusingly, and he sighed.

'So were you. I was trying to call you. The babies are getting restless.'

'Oh. Sorry. I'm done.'

She told him where she was, and he looked at the map, worked out where he was and then made his way there through the teaming throng of happy shoppers.

Well, he was happy, too—or he had been, till she'd bitten his head off for nothing. Oh, well. He supposed she had some justification for thinking he was using the phone for work purposes, because he *had* made one quick call to Andrea. But only the one, and it had lasted three minutes tops, and it had been important.

So he couldn't get on his self-righteous high horse and rip her head off right back, because she'd been right. He had cheated, and she was probably right not to trust him.

He found her, standing near a till with an armful of clothes, waiting for him.

'I'm sorry,' she said, her first words, and he felt a little prickle of guilt.

'Don't worry about it,' he said. 'So—what did you buy?'

She didn't know what to wear.

He'd called into the supermarket on the way home, left her and the babies in the car, and run in to do a shop. He'd been less than five minutes, so she had no idea what he'd bought, but he had a small carrier with him.

'What's that?' she asked, and he grinned.

'Supper. I'm cooking for you.'

'Really?' Oh, lord, that sounded dreadful, but she could still smell the garlic on her skin after the paella, and she had no idea what he would go for this time.

'Don't worry, there's no garlic,' he promised with a wry grin, and she laughed self-consciously.

'Sorry. So what are we having?'

'Aha,' he said, tapping the side of his nose. 'I'm cooking. All you have to do is put on something pretty and be entertained.'

So here she was, washed and spruced, wearing a light touch of make-up for the first time in months, and standing naked in her bedroom contemplating her purchases.

A jumper, she thought, being chicken, but she'd heard him light the fire in the sitting room, and when she'd popped down for something for the girls she'd noticed he'd laid the table in the kitchen rather than the chilly and more formal dining-room.

So she wouldn't be cold.

So—one of the new tops? The lacy one with the tiny camisole underneath, perhaps? Or the silky one with the little collar and the fine embroidery?

Lacy, she decided, and that dictated the bra and pants set, because of the colour combination. She'd only bought one pair of trousers, but they fitted her so well she was delighted with them, and she put them on to complete the outfit, stood back to look at herself, and blinked.

Wow. That was a bit different.

Gone were the jeans with the slightly grubby knees from spending her life on the floor with the babies, and the jumper with a little stain on the front from some tomato-and-pasta baby food that didn't seem to want to wash out.

Gone, too, the dark rims round her eyes and the tired, straggly hair.

Instead she looked feminine, elegant and—yes—pretty. And it made her feel a million dollars.

In a fit of wickedness, she squirted scent into the air and walked through it, then slipped on her high heels and went downstairs.

He was sitting at the table flicking through a magazine, and he looked up and his jaw sagged.

'Wow,' he breathed, and, standing up, he put the magazine on one side and walked over to her, his eyes never leaving her. 'Turn round,' he instructed, with an edge in his voice, and she turned, slowly, and then came back to face him and met his eyes. His smouldering, fire-blue eyes. How could blue ever be a cold colour? Not on Max. Oh, no.

'Will I do?' she asked a little self-consciously, and his mouth twitched into a lopsided grin.

'Oh, I think you'll do,' he said, his voice slightly gruff and gravelly, the way it was when he was aroused, and the words stroked through her like fire, sensitising every spot they touched. He stood there for another few seconds, studying her, then with another crooked smile he stepped back and held out a chair for her. 'Would you care to take a seat, madam?'

'Thank you.'

She smiled up at him, laughing when he flicked a napkin across her lap with a flourish. It would have had more impact if it hadn't been a tea towel, but his mouth just twitched and he went over to the stove, set the griddle on it and watched it until it was smoking, then dropped two dark steaks on it.

She sniffed the air. Tuna? Her stomach rumbled, and she looked for the plates. Ah. There they were, just coming out of the bottom oven with a bowl of new potatoes. He put a knob of butter on the potatoes, sprinkled them with chopped chives and set them on the table, dished up the tuna steaks and set her plate in front of her with another of those flourishes which she realised were becoming part of the meal.

'Salad, madam?'

'Thank you. Murphy, in your bed, this isn't for you. Max, sit down.'

'I'm not sure that doesn't put me in the same

category as the dog,' he said with irony, and she chuckled.

'Of course not. Good boy.'

Giving a little snort, he sat opposite her, and then got up, lit the candle in the middle of the table and turned down the lights. 'Better,' he said, and handed her the potatoes. 'No garlic, please note.'

'Chilli?'

He shrugged. 'Just a touch—sweet chilli and lime marinade. It shouldn't be hot.'

It wasn't. It was delicious, cooked to perfection and utterly gorgeous, and she was more than ready for it. The wine was a delicate rosé, not so chilled that the flavour was lost, and he followed it with little individual chocolate pots, ready made but wickedness itself, decorated with fresh strawberries and served with a dark, rich Cabernet that was the perfect complement.

'Wow, Max, that was fabulous,' she said, pushing her plate away and smiling at him in amazement.

To her surprise, he coloured slightly and gave a wry, self-conscious grin. 'Thank you. I just—read the instructions.'

'No, you did much more than that. You went

to a lot of trouble to make it right, and it was wonderful. Thank you.'

His smile was warm and did funny things to her insides. 'It's a pleasure,' he said, and she could tell he meant it. 'Coffee in the sitting room?'

'That would be lovely.'

'Go on, then, go and sit down.'

'What about this lot?'

He shrugged. 'What about it? It won't come to any harm. Come on, out of here. I'll stack the dishwasher while the kettle boils, if that'll make you happier. Now, shoo.'

She shooed, going into the sitting room with Murphy and putting another log on the fire, then sitting down on the sofa to wait for him. Murphy was sniffing the table, and she pushed him gently out of the way with her foot and looked at the little dish he'd been investigating.

Truffles? Yum. She had one, just to pass the time, and then Max arrived with the tray and gave Murphy a chew to eat by the fire. 'I thought it might keep him out of the chocolates.'

'It will. But only till he's eaten it.'

'Well, we'll have to finish them first,' he said, taking the seat beside her and handing her her coffee. 'Here—open wide.'

And he put one of the wicked little truffles into her mouth.

'Mmm. They're gorgeous,' she said. Well, she meant to say. It came out a little more garbled than that, and she got the giggles, and he shook his head and slung his arm casually around the back of the sofa behind her and grinned.

'Oh, dear. Did you have two whole glasses of wine?' he teased.

'No, I did not,' she retorted, recovering her composure and poking him in the ribs. 'Cheeky.'

'Two halves, anyway. What did you think of them?'

'Lovely. They were really nice. I bet they didn't come from the bargain bucket.'

He chuckled. 'Not exactly. But I felt it was worth it.' He trailed a finger down her cheek, and smiled a little wryly. 'You know, I thought you looked gorgeous this morning, but now…'

His finger dipped, trailing round the neckline of her top, following the edge down towards her cleavage, and she felt the air jam in her lungs.

'Max.'

His hand dropped away and he straightened up, lounging back in his corner of the sofa and reaching for his coffee. She leant over and picked up a chocolate, and he said, 'My turn,' and opened his mouth. Just slightly, just enough so that, when she put the truffle in between his teeth, his lips brushed her fingers, the slightly moist surface catching her skin so that when she took her hand away his lips clung softly to her fingertips.

Her eyes flew up to his, hot and dark and dangerous, and she felt need flow like molten lava through her veins.

His hand came up and caught hold of hers, easing it from his mouth and placing it against his heart, and she could feel the pounding beat beneath her palm, the taut muscles, the coiled tension in him.

And she wanted him.

Now. Tonight.

'Max?' she whispered.

He was staring at her mouth, his eyes slightly glazed, and she could see the pulse beating in his throat. His eyes flicked up to hers and locked.

'Take me to bed.'

CHAPTER EIGHT

'ARE you sure?'

'Yes.'

With a sharp hiss of indrawn breath, his eyes flickered briefly shut, then opened, locking with hers, burning in their intensity, and he got slowly to his feet and held out his hand, pulling her up so she was standing facing him, just inches away but not quite touching.

'You don't have to do this.'

'I know.'

He closed his eyes and said something she couldn't hear, then turned away. 'We need to put this lot away and sort the dog out.'

'I'll do it.'

'No. We'll both do it. It'll be quicker.' He put everything back on the tray and carried it out to the kitchen, Murphy close behind him, and he took the dog out while she put the milk back in the fridge and checked that all the food was out of Murphy's reach. It was—all except the chocolates.

Max came back in with the dog, picked up the truffles and met her eyes. 'I'll bring these,' he said, and she was instantly taken back to another time, another place, when he'd brought chocolates to bed and fed them to her, one by one, as he'd made love to her.

She could still taste them.

'Don't look at me like that,' he said, his voice taut, 'or I'll lose it completely.' His lips quirked in a fleeting smile, but she could feel the tension coming off him in waves. It matched her own, and suddenly she couldn't wait any more.

Turning on her heel, she walked out of the kitchen, flicking off the light and leaving him to follow.

She heard him murmur to the dog, close the door, and then she could feel him right behind her, the warmth of his body just a breath away.

'Your room or mine?'

'Mine. It's further from the babies.'

Only just, but she wasn't at all sure, after so long, that she'd be able to keep a lid on her reaction to his love-making—and the shower at work hadn't been the only time he'd made her scream. Not by a long way.

She turned on the light, but he'd brought the candle, and he put it on the chest of drawers beside the chocolates, lit it and turned out the light. She was grateful for that, because it suddenly dawned on her that he hadn't seen her body since she'd had the babies, and, between the ravages of breastfeeding, the scar from the C-section and the gain in weight, maybe he needed a rather more subtle introduction to the new her.

But it seemed he wasn't in any hurry to take her clothes off after all. Instead he tunnelled his fingers through her hair, bent his head and touched his lips to hers.

Just a feather touch, the lightest brushing of skin on skin, but, as he moved his head from side to side, their lips clung, dragging gently, heightening the sensation, until she felt a whimper force its way out of her throat.

Oh, Max, kiss me, she begged silently, and, as if he'd heard her, he anchored her head more firmly with his hands and stroked his tongue across her lips, coaxing them apart.

They needed no coaxing. She opened to him, and with a ragged groan he slanted his mouth over her and plundered it, his mouth hungry on hers, searching, thrusting, his tongue duelling with hers, driving her wild.

Only when they had to break for breath did he lift his head, the air sawing in and out of his lungs, his eyes glittering in the candlelight. 'Jules, I need you,' he whispered, his voice rough and urgent.

'I need you, too—please, Max. Now.'

And without any further delay he stripped off his shirt, shucked his trousers and socks and heeled off his shoes in one motion.

The boxers hid nothing, the soft jersey clinging faithfully to his erection, and she felt her mouth dry. It had been so long. Her body was trembling, the need so great she could hardly move, but it was all right, because she didn't need to. He was there, his hands gently, carefully easing the top over her head—first the lace, then the little camisole—and when he saw the bra he closed his eyes briefly and she saw his lips move soundlessly.

'Thank God you didn't show me that in the shop,' he said at last, and she laughed a little breathlessly.

'There's more,' she said, and he groaned and slid the zip down on her trousers and eased them away.

She sucked her stomach in, but he tutted and ran his hand over it, his hot, dry palm flat against the skin, his fingers trailing fire. One finger flicked at the elastic of her little lace shorts. 'What are these?' he said, his voice unsteady.

'I thought you might like them.'

'You're going to kill me,' he whispered, and, drawing her into his arms, he brought their bodies into contact for the first time.

They both gasped, then sighed, and then eased closer, until finally he lifted his head and met her eyes.

'Jules—I have to have you now, or I'm going to die, I swear it,' he said unevenly. 'I need you so damned much.'

His eyes were bright with fire, and his chest was heaving against hers, the candlelight picking out the sharp definition of his muscles and turning him to gold as he lifted her gently in his arms and laid her on the bed.

He followed her down, his eyes never leaving her face, and then finally he let them track over her, following the line of his hands as they stroked over her skin and left fire in their wake. He ran his knuckles over the edge of her bra, down the line of her cleavage, then turned his hand and cupped her breast, his thumb chafing lightly over her nipple until she thought she'd scream.

'I want to taste you,' he muttered gruffly. 'Every day I watch the babies suckle from you, and…'

She wanted it, too. Ached for it. She undid the catch—front-fastening, she'd thought, for convenience, but she wondered now if she'd had this in mind all along—and he eased the cups away, then slid his hand inside and lifted one breast to his lips.

Milk dewed on her nipple, and he caught it on his tongue and tasted it, then closed his mouth over her and suckled hard.

She gasped, a shaft of white-hot need lancing through her with deadly accuracy, and he lifted his head, his eyes black now, his mouth taut.

For the longest moment they stayed like that, their eyes locked, and then with a desperate sound he stripped away her tiny lace shorts, ripped off his boxers and moved over her, his solid, muscled thighs hard against her legs as he nudged them apart.

'Jules,' he whispered.

And then he was there, inside her, filling her, and she felt the storm closing round them, the sensation overwhelming her until suddenly everything broke loose and her climax ripped through her.

He caught her scream in his mouth, trapped it against the savage groan that tore from his chest. And then he rolled her to her side and pulled her in close to him, their bodies still locked together, their hearts racing, and, when she finally opened her eyes, he was looking at her with wonder in his eyes, the lashes clumped with tears.

'I love you,' he whispered, and, drawing her close again, he tucked her head under his chin and wrapped his arms around her, his hands stroking slowly, rhythmically, against her spine until finally she fell asleep in his arms.

He'd missed her so much.

He'd never told her, hadn't revealed just how hellish the last year had been. Oh, he'd said a few things, but nothing compared to what was locked up in his heart.

But she was back now, and, if it killed him, he'd make sure he didn't fail her again.

His arm was going dead, but he didn't want to disturb her. He was just enjoying the luxury of holding her, and he wasn't sure how she'd be when she woke up. Distant? Full of regret?

Hell, he hoped not.

And then she stirred, opened her eyes and smiled at him, and he felt the tension ease out of him like a punctured balloon.

'Hi.'

'Hi,' he answered, and feathered a kiss across her lips. 'You all right?'

'Mmm. You?'

'Oh, yes. I'm very all right.'

'My leg's dead.'

'Snap. My arm's fallen off, I think.'

'It's going to hurt.'

'Uh-huh.'

She grinned. 'One, two, three—'

He gave a little groan and shifted further out of her way, then laughed and drew her back in to his side, so they lay with fingers intertwined and their heads together on the pillow. 'Better?'

'Mmm. Max?'

'Yes?'

'I love you.'

'Oh, Jules.' He rolled towards her, not caring about the pins and needles in his arm, and kissed her gently. 'I love you, too.'

'Good,' she murmured, and, a second later, he heard a soft, almost imperceptible snore.

He smiled. He'd tease her about that in the morning, he thought, and, shifting closer to her, he curled his hand over her hip and went to sleep.

* * *

The babies woke her, and she rolled to her back, opened her eyes and blinked.

It was broad daylight, and she could hear Max's voice in their room. Getting out of bed and wincing at the unaccustomed aches, she pulled her dressing gown on hastily and went out to them.

'Hello, my lovelies,' she said, going into the room, and they beamed at her from their cots.

'Am I included in that?' he asked, looking much too sexy for his own good in nothing but a pair of boxers, and she chuckled.

'You might be. How long have they been awake?'

'A few minutes. I've changed their nappies and given them a bottle of juice, but I think they want their mum and something rather more substantial.'

'I'm sure they do. Come on, my little ones. Shall we go downstairs and say hello to Murphy?'

She lifted Ava out of her cot and handed her to Max, and then pulled Libby up into her arms and nuzzled her. 'Hello, tinker. Are you going to be good today?'

'Probably not, if she's like her sister,' he said drily, and carried her downstairs. 'I'll do that stairgate this morning.'

'Mmm. Please. I'd hate anything to happen. Hello, Smurfs! How are you, boy? Find anything nice to eat?'

'I'm sure he will have given it his best shot,' Max said wryly. 'Won't you, you old rascal?'

Murphy thumped and wagged and grinned at him, and she laughed. 'He's such a suck-up. Horrid dog, aren't you? Horrid. Here, Libby, go to Daddy.'

'Da-dad,' she said, and they both stopped in their tracks.

'Did I dream that?' she asked, and he laughed and shrugged his shoulders.

'Only if I did, too. I thought Ava said "Da-da" yesterday, but then I thought she was just babbling.'

'Da-da!' Ava chirruped from the playpen, hanging onto the edge and grinning furiously at him, and Julia felt her eyes fill with tears.

'They said your name,' she whispered, pressing her hand to her mouth, and he swallowed and grinned, and looked as if he'd crow at any minute.

'Well, girls. How about that?' he said, and put the kettle on.

Breakfast was over, they were all washed and dressed, and Max was trying not to think about the fact that he couldn't take Jules back to bed for hours. Unless the girls had a sleep in the afternoon, of course.

'Shall we do some house-hunting?' he suggested to take his mind off it.

'Sure. If I get the computer we can do it in here. We've got wireless.' And she disappeared and came back a moment later with a laptop. John Blake's?

No. Don't get funny about it. He's given your family a home.

'Shove up,' she said, and settled herself down on the sofa with the laptop. She keyed in a password, and he hated himself for memorising it without thinking. Hell, she was right not to trust him, he thought.

'OK. I'm on one of the big property sites. What are we looking for, and how much?'

'I wouldn't put an upper limit on it. Start at the top and work down.'

'Really?'

'Well—yeah. Why not? Do you want to live in something horrible?'

'No! I want to live in something normal!' she retorted, and he sighed.

Wrong again. Two steps forward, three back, he thought, and wondered why he could never seem to get it right for more than a few minutes at a time.

'Just put in the area you're interested in, and let's see what there is.'

Nothing. That was the simple answer. There was nothing that wasn't either too small or too remote or too pushed-in or just plain wrong.

And nothing, but nothing, matched up to Rose Cottage.

'I wish I could stay here,' she said unhappily.

'He wouldn't sell it?'

'Would you want it?'

He smiled at her wryly. 'It's not really up to me, is it? We're talking about your home, your choice, somewhere for you and the babies. And I guess all I'll do is visit you.'

Her eyes clouded, and she looked hastily away.

Now what? 'Unless I work away during the week and come back for weekends. I'm not really into commuting. I'd rather work a short week.'

'What—only six days, you mean, instead of seven?'

He sighed. 'Can we start again?'

She looked away and bit her lips. 'Sorry. It's just—we seem to be getting on so well, and then the future rears its ugly head and there's no way round it.'

And the babies were fussing and bored.

'Let's dress them up and go for a walk,' he suggested. 'We could use the slings.'

They'd bought slings the day before, to carry the babies on their fronts so they could go for walks without taking the buggy, and so they sorted them out. He ended up with Ava and Julia with Libby.

They swapped them all the time, he realised, as if neither of them wanted to create a closer bond with just one of the twins. Odd, how it had just happened and they hadn't talked about it, but then it had always been like that with them. They'd hardly ever needed to discuss things, they'd just agreed.

Until now, and it seemed that sharing the babies equally was the only thing they could agree on.

Well, out of bed, at least. That, he was relieved to know, was still as amazing as ever. And he wasn't going to think about it now.

They strolled along the riverbank for a way, while Murphy rushed around and sniffed things and dug a few furious holes in search of some poor water-vole or other unfortunate creature, and then they walked back to the house.

'Do any of these barns belong to the house?' he asked, and she nodded.

'Yes, all of them. It was a farm—Rose Farm—but the farmland was all sold off and they took the name, so it was renamed Rose Cottage. Which is silly, really, because it's a bit big to be a cottage, but there you go.'

He looked around curiously. There were lots of buildings that were too small to do anything specific with, but others—like the range of open-fronted, single-storey brick cart-lodges— could be converted into office accommodation.

If only they could find something like it for sale, then there was a possibility that he could work from home. Not just him, but one or two other members of the team—a sort of satellite office. He knew lots of people who'd scaled down their operations and 'gone rural', as one of them had put it, but he'd never seen the attraction.

Until now.

'Come and see the garden,' she said, and led him through the gate at the side.

He'd been out there with the dog, of course, but he'd never really examined it, and, as she walked him through it and talked about it, he began to see it through her eyes.

And it was beautiful. A little ragged round the edges, of course, in the middle of winter, but even now there were daffodils and crocuses coming up, and buds were forming on the rose bushes, and, if he looked hard, he could imagine it in summer.

'I've got photos of it with the roses all flowering,' she said. 'It's stunning.'

It would be. He could see that. And he remembered what she'd said, on the day that she'd left him.

I want...a house, a garden, time to potter amongst the plants, to stick my fingers in the soil and smell the roses... We never stop and smell the roses, Max. Never.

Well, she had her garden now, and her roses. Watching her talk about them, he could see the change in her, the glow in her eyes, the warmth in her skin, the life in her. Real life, not just the adrenaline high of another conquest, but genuine satisfaction and contentment.

And what shocked him more than any of that was that he wanted it, too.

'Why don't you have a day out with Jane?'

'What?' She shifted forward on the sofa and stared down at him on the floor; he was lying at right angles to her with his hands linked behind his head and Libby sprawled asleep on his stomach.

'You heard. I'll look after the girls. We'll be fine.'

'Are you sure?' she asked doubtfully.

'Yeah, we'll be great. Don't you trust me?'

'Well, of course I trust you. I'm just not sure you know what you're letting yourself in for.'

'Undiluted hell, I expect, but I'm sure we'll all survive.'

She thought about it, and shook her head. 'No. But I might meet her for a coffee,' she suggested, toning it all down a little and going for something more manageable. 'Besides, she's got the baby, and the others will need dropping off at school and picking up again, and she's always really busy. But I'll ask her. When were you thinking of?'

'Whenever you like. Tomorrow?'

Tomorrow was Monday. One week since he'd arrived. It was two days since they'd ended up in bed. And it had been incredible, but she was letting herself get too addicted to it, and there were other things to think about. Like him in London and her here with the children.

Still, it could work. Lots of couples did it.

But she didn't want to! She wanted it all! And she was realistic enough to know she wasn't going to get it. Not with Max, and the thought of having a relationship with anyone else was just a joke. There was no way anyone could live up to Max. It wouldn't be fair to ask them to. And, besides, she loved him. Desperately.

She just had to find a way to make it work, for all their sakes.

'I'll go and ring her,' she said, tucking a cushion down next to Ava so she couldn't roll off the sofa, and getting carefully to her feet.

'Julia? How are you? I've been afraid to ask!'

'Oh, a bit like the curate's egg—good in parts.' Very good, but she didn't want to talk about those parts. And the bad bits—well, they were too difficult to contemplate. 'Look, Max has offered to babysit for me so we can grab a coffee. What are you doing tomorrow?'

'Nothing I can't cancel. I'm dying to see you and hear all about it. Where, and what time?'

'The Barn? Ten-thirty?'

'Fine. How long will you have?'

'As long as I want. He offered me the day, but I don't want him having a bad experience so he's put off for life.'

'No, absolutely not. Clever girl. Right, let's make it ten-thirty tomorrow, and I'll tell Pete I'll be home at one. He's at home, so he can babysit. Does that sound OK?'

'Fine,' she said, and hung up with a smile. She was really looking forward to it. It would be the first chance she'd had to see Jane on their own since she'd left hospital with the babies, and she was ridiculously excited.

She went back to the sitting room and found him lying on his front, with Libby on her back just under his head, giggling while he blew raspberries on her tummy. He looked round over his shoulder, and she stopped admiring his muscular bottom and smiled at him.

'It's all arranged. I'm meeting her tomorrow at ten-thirty at a coffee shop by a craft centre just a couple of miles away, and I'll be back at one. Is that OK?'

'Fine. Good. We'll be all right, won't we, half-pint?' he said, grinning and turning back to Libby, so Julia was free to admire his really rather gorgeous bottom without interruption.

'So tell me all! I've been so worried about you.'

'No, you just want the low-down,' Julia teased, settling down with a proper, decent latte and a properly indecent slab of chocolate-fudge cake.

'Well, of course I want the low-down,' Jane said, exasperated, and, reaching over with her coffee spoon, she stuck it in the cake and stole a huge chunk. 'Mmm. Oh, wow.'

Or something like it. Julia rolled her eyes and took a slightly less disgusting chunk for herself.

'Well?' Jane asked when her mouth was available again.

'Well—I don't know. Sometimes I think it's going all right, and other times— Well, he cheats a bit.'

'Cheats?'

'Not like that. We had rules. Two weeks—no phone calls, no Internet access, no sneaking back to London or staying up all night working—and most of the time he's been great. But he tried to sneak his phone back—he rang it from mine, and I think he was hoping to hear it and track it down, but I had it under my pillow on silent, and I answered it and told him off.'

'Oops.'

'Yeah. And we were looking on the Internet over the weekend for a house for me. Max is a bit funny about me living in another man's house, and if he wants to buy me one…' She shrugged. 'But we couldn't find anything round here that ticked all our boxes. Well, mine really, because, as he says, he'll be in London and I want to be near my friends. And that's the problem, of course. He won't live here—can't, really, working the hours he does—and I won't go back to London until I'm absolutely sure that he's in earnest about this and in it for the long haul. It's a bit like going on a crash diet—you can do it for a few days, but then something crops up.'

'Like chocolate-fudge cake,' Jane said, eyeing it longingly, so that Julia pushed it towards her and handed her the fork.

'Like chocolate-fudge cake, or an unmissable deal or a stock-market crisis, and he'll be off, I know he will. And I don't know if I can deal with it. I don't want to be a single parent, but I'd rather do that than live in a constant state of flux.'

'And have you told him that?'

'Oh, yes. But what can he do?'

Jane shrugged, stole another bit of cake and handed it back. 'Feel free to tell me to butt out and all that, but does he actually need to work? I mean, to live? For money?'

'No. Absolutely not. He doesn't ever need to work again. But he'd go crazy. He's an adrenaline junkie. He can't live without the cut and thrust.'

'Talking of which,' Jane said with a wicked twinkle in her eye, 'you're looking all loved-up at the moment. I take it *that* part of the reconciliation is going well?'

Julie felt a tide of colour sweep over her cheeks. 'That,' she said, stabbing her chocolatey fork at her friend, 'is none of your darned business.'

'That's a yes, then. Thank goodness for that.'

'Why?'

'Because he's the sexiest man alive! Don't get me wrong, I adore Pete, but your Max is seriously hot, and it would be such a wicked waste.'

She sighed. 'That's part of the problem, of course. If he looked like the back end of a bus and couldn't make love for nuts, it would be easier to leave him.'

'But you don't want to leave him,' Jane pointed out reasonably. 'You just want to live with him somewhere that isn't in the flightpath of his next plane out. You just have to work out a way to keep him with you.'

She rolled her eyes. 'And I can do that by…?'

'How about him moving the office out here?'

'What?'

'You heard. Lots of people are doing it. Or he could work from home.'

'If he could work from home, he wouldn't be in New York or Tokyo all the time.'

'Ah, but there's a difference between wanting to and being able to. He's able to work from home. He just hasn't wanted to yet. That's the crux of it. Are you going to eat any more of that?'

'You should have just had your own,' she said, sliding the plate back to Jane.

'Nah-ah. I'm on a diet.'

'Yeah, right. So—you think I should find a way to keep him in the country?'

'Mmm. Apart from just handcuffing him to the bed, which of course is the other option.'

She laughed into her coffee, splattering herself with froth and getting the giggles. 'You're incorrigible. It's so nice to see you again like this,' she said with a sigh, mopping up the last of the coffee. 'If only I didn't have to move so soon. You know John's coming back in a month or so, and I've got to find somewhere else to live?'

'No,' Jane said, shaking her head.

'Yes, he is.'

'No, he isn't. He's met someone. Hasn't he told you? Some guy in Chicago who's fifteen years younger and wants him to move out there permanently. But he's torn.'

'About the guy?'

'No, that's pretty certain. About Murphy, I think. If it wasn't for the dog, he'd do it, but you know how he adores him. And the cottage. But the dog's the real deal-breaker.'

'So—if he stays,' she said slowly, 'Then what will he do with the cottage?'

Jane shrugged. 'Sell it, I suppose. I don't know. I didn't speak to him, it was Pete who answered the phone last night while I was in the bath. That's all I know. It was pretty late, that's probably why he didn't ring you. Why don't you ring him?'

'I might,' she said. 'I might very well do that. How far behind us is Chicago? Is it six hours?'

'Something like that.'

'So, by the time I get home, it'll only be seven am. That's a bit early.'

'And you might want to talk to Max.'

'Or not. I might want to present him with a neatly packaged solution, and see how hard he tries to get out of it. It's easy to talk about in theory, but, when it comes to the crunch, I might get a more honest response if he can see it in black and white and has to make a decision one way or the other. If he feels cornered, then it won't work, and at least I'll know.'

And please God it wouldn't come to that.

CHAPTER NINE

THERE was nothing.

He pushed the chair away from the desk, glared at the screen in frustration and wondered what on earth he was going to do about finding them a house where they could all live while they sorted this out.

Although he had no real idea if he could sort it out. He'd need to get into some serious discussion with his team before he made any radical changes, but in the meantime—

'Gallagher.'

'Hello? Who's that?'

Max stared at the phone in his hand, realising he'd answered it on autopilot. 'Um—it's Max Gallagher. Can I help you?'

'Probably not. Can I speak to Julia, please?'

The voice was cautious, and he glanced at the caller display and saw it was an international call. Blake?

'I'm sorry, she's not in. I'm babysitting the girls. It's—ah—it's her husband.'

'I wondered. It's John Blake—she's housesitting for me.'

'Yes. Yes, I gather. Look, she'll be back at one, if you want to speak to her. She's gone for coffee with Jane.'

'Ah. Right. Well, in which case she'll probably know, but I was phoning to tell her that I'm not coming back. Well, I don't think so. There are—um—personal reasons, and— Well, I've met someone and I'm going to be living here, so I needed to discuss the house with her. And the dog.'

Murphy.

Max glanced down at him, lying on his foot as usual, and wondered what his plans were for the dog. He discovered, to his surprise, that it really mattered to him.

'I don't suppose you want to sell the house to me?'

'To *you*?'

'Yes—for Julia. We're—' Hell, he hated doing their washing in public, but he guessed Blake would know about their marital problems, at least in outline. 'We're trying to sort out—see if there's a way…'

'Is she all right with that?'

'Oh, there are rules,' he said with irony. 'We're halfway through a "no contact with the office" trial at the moment. But I can't just cut myself off from work, and I've been looking to see if there's anywhere around here where I can have a home office with a few staff, and a home with my family, so I can spend at least the majority of my time with them. And there's nothing.'

'And you think you could do that with my place?'

'Subject to the planners playing ball.'

'They like that,' John Blake confirmed. 'They don't like barn conversions for housing, but, for rural enterprise and business use, they're usually quite keen. And, if it's for your own personal business use, they might be very cooperative. In fact I've had some plans drawn up. They're probably still in the filing cabinet. You could have a look at them.'

'So—does that mean you'd consider selling to me?' he asked cautiously.

'I don't know,' the man said. 'I've got a problem with that. I seem to have a sitting tenant, and I want her to be happy with her new landlord, so I'd have to talk to her.'

He gave a soft laugh. 'Oh, I think she'd be happy. She's been saying that she doesn't want to move, and I can see that she really loves it here. And—there's the matter of the dog.'

'Yes.'

Max smiled thoughtfully. 'But we love Murphy, don't we, mate?' he said, rubbing the dog's ears so that he thumped his tail.

'Is he there with you?'

'He's always here with me. He's lying on my foot.'

'And you'd keep him?'

He laughed. 'I think Julia would kill me before she let anything else happen to him. And, besides, he's good company on a run.'

'Oh, you run? He loves that. He always comes with me when I go out.'

'So will you consider it?'

'We'd need to fix a fair price. Can you set that up—get a couple of the local agents round to value it?' He suggested two names, and Max jotted them down.

'Give me your number, too.'

He wrote it beside the names of the agents, then added, 'Can you do me a favour, John? Can you keep this a secret from Julia for a few days? Just to give me time to see if it'll work.'

'If you're taking the dog, the price is negotiable.'

He laughed softly. 'John, we'll take the dog whatever. I can't imagine being without him, and I like the idea of her having a dog with her when I'm not around. I meant the planners. I need to get an unofficial nod from them, some kind of informal agreement that they'd consider it favourably before I could go ahead, but I don't want to raise Julia's hopes.'

'OK, I'll wait until I hear from you. But I have to warn you, I spoke to Pete last night so Jane may well have told her that I'm staying over here. Just so you know.'

'OK. I'll stall her—tell her there's plenty of time to think about it. I'll dream up something. Shall I get her to call you when she's back?'

'If you could. Thanks. And give Murphy a hug from me.'

He chuckled. 'Will do.'

He hung up, stared at the phone for a second and then grinned. 'Well, Smurphs, we might have got ourselves a house. What do you think of that?'

His tail thumped, and Max found the number of the local planning office and called them.

Ten minutes later, he had his unofficial answer, and it was a guarded and conditional yes. He punched the air, checked the babies, made himself another coffee, went back to the study and called Andrea.

'We need a meeting,' he said. 'I've got something to put to you. And I want Stephen there.'

'When are you thinking of?'

'This afternoon. Sort it.'

'What about Julia?'

'This is for Julia. I'm trying to find a way that we can be together, and that depends to a certain extent on you guys. You could do me a favour. Call her and tell her I need to get down to the office and sort out a major crisis. Make something up. I don't care, just don't tell her what this is about. I want it to be a surprise.'

'Andrea?'

'Hi, Julia. Look, I hate to do this to you, but I'm afraid I need Max back here at the office as soon as possible. There's a problem, and he's the only one with all the information to sort it out. You know what he's like for carrying things in his head.'

'Don't I just? It used to drive me mad. OK. I'll send him back to you. Do you need to talk to him?'

Max was looking at her curiously, and she

shook her head at him. 'OK, Andrea. Thanks. I'll pass it on.'

She hung up and looked across at him again. 'Andrea wants you to go down—there's a hiccup. Apparently you keep too much in your head, so they can't sort it. Now where have I heard that before?'

'Can I go?'

She pretended to sigh, but secretly she was delighted. She wanted to call John, but she didn't want Max to know, so if he was out of the way...

'I think you have to, don't you? Go on, Max. Just go and get it over with.'

'You're a star. And I'm sorry.'

He kissed her goodbye, and it was only after he'd gone that she realised he seemed quite keen to go. Had he set it up with Andrea while she was out? She picked up the phone and looked at the last number called, but it was Jane. The only other phone was in the study, so she went in and checked on that one.

A local number, one she didn't recognise. She pressed redial, and discovered it was an estate agent.

'Sorry, I must have dialled the wrong number,' she said, and put the phone down again, smiling.

So Max was househunting, was he? Interesting. Well, she'd have to make sure he didn't do anything hasty. She could always veto anything he came up with if John was willing to sell. She just had to find that out.

She rang him.

'Hey, you old dark horse, I gather congratulations are in order!'

'Ah. Jane told you. Yes—and thank you.'

'So I take it you're happy?'

'Oh, yes. His name's Ryan, and he's forty-two and he's an architect. And he has an amazing house, and he wants me to share it with him. And we're going to have a ceremony, so, if you'd be able to join us, we'd be just over the moon.'

'Oh, John! I'm so pleased for you!' she said, her eyes filling. He was such a nice man, and he deserved happiness. 'Murphs will miss you, but I don't want you to worry about him. I'll keep him with me. The girls love him to bits, and I couldn't bear to part with him, so you can't have him even if you want him!'

John laughed. 'That's OK. Ryan has dogs, so I still get my share of dog hair in the food. I feel really at home.'

She chuckled, then bit her lip. 'John, I want to ask you something. My—um—my husband's back in the frame. Max. He tracked me down—

I didn't realise it would be so hard to find me, and I wasn't really hiding, just avoiding the issue—but he's back with me, and we're trying to find a way forward. And I want us to have a home, out here in the country, near all my friends, because I know he's going to have to go away on business. But I was thinking, if you'd sell us the house, there are all the barns. He could have an office here.'

'Yes.'

'What?'

'Yes, I'll sell you the house. Of course I will, if it'll make you happy.'

'Oh.' That was quick. 'Really?'

'Really. And I'm really glad to hear you're getting back together. Just hearing you talk about him for the last year made me think you should be together. You obviously love him very deeply, and, if this helps you to find a way to overcome your problems, well then I'm with you all the way.'

'Oh, John, thank you. I can't tell you what it means to me.' She felt a flicker of excitement start deep down inside, and spread until her whole body was glowing with it. 'We'll have to have it valued. I could call some estate agents.'

'Don't bother. I've got a friend there with an

agency. He knows the house well. He'll give us a fair figure, and I'm happy to go with that if you are. I'll get onto him.'

'Sure. Fine—of course.' And that meant she wouldn't have the problem of getting Max out of the way.

'Let me know the moment you've spoken to him, could you? And, if you ring and Max answers, don't tell him, will you? I want it to be a surprise.'

John chuckled. 'OK. I'll call you when I've got a figure. How are my babies?'

'Gorgeous. And into everything. Max has had to fix a stairgate because they're crawling everywhere, and Ava's trying to walk—and I have to go, John, because she's trying to get out of the playpen! I'll speak to you soon. Love you.'

'Love you, too, chicken. Take care.'

She rescued Ava, picked up the phone again and tucked it in her pocket, picked Libby up and carried them both through to the sitting room. 'No climbing,' she warned them, and, tipping out a pile of toys on the floor, she sat on the edge of the sofa and phoned Jane to tell her the news.

'So—that's what I hope to do. And I know it's totally out of the blue—but, well, if it's not what you want I'll quite understand. I'll need a good, reliable team at my head office, and I don't know how realistic it would be to relocate everyone out to the country, so at the moment I'm just sounding people out.'

Andrea and Stephen were silent. They looked dumbfounded, and he realised he'd been jumping the gun, getting carried along on a tidal wave of theory again, not thinking about the effect it would have on everyone else.

He was good at that, he thought in disgust, and shook his head.

'Sorry. It's a crazy idea. Forget it.'

'Actually, no. I don't want to forget it,' Stephen said, suddenly coming to life. 'We don't need to be in London. Communication is worldwide and simplicity itself. And Dana's been talking about getting out of London. If it wasn't for the fact that the hours are too long for commuting, we would have done it before. But, now we've got the baby, we were talking about buying two places and shifting her and the baby out to the country with me joining them whenever I can. But this could be even better. This could really work for me.'

Wow. He nodded thoughtfully, and shifted his gaze to Andrea.

'Any comments?'

'I can't move. My daughter's about to have a baby, and she needs me close. She's disabled, so it's not easy.'

'And she lives in London?'

'Yes. Well, just outside. Her husband's a pilot. He flies out of Stansted. They live near Stratford, so I can get to them on the Tube.'

'Would they contemplate a move? Stansted's only an hour from the village, probably less. Forty minutes? It's only just in Suffolk, on the Suffolk-Essex border. It's not a million miles from here. And I'd make sure you had a generous relocation package.'

She frowned. 'And them?'

'All of you. Whatever it takes, Andrea. If we were to move the entire operation—and bearing in mind I want to cut back to something much more manageable, for all our sakes—then I'll need my key people.'

'I've only worked for you for six months, Max. How can I be so key?'

He gave a wry laugh. 'You have no idea,' he said drily. 'I am not an easy man to work for.'

She smiled. 'I had noticed. You just need managing.'

'So Jules tells me.' He glanced at his watch.

'Look, I need to get back. Can I leave it with you to think about? And, if you feel we can get enough key people on board, then I'll call a meeting and throw it open for discussion with the rest of the team. And I don't want Jules to know anything about this until I have something concrete to tell her.'

'So how can we contact you?'

He gave Andrea a sly smile. 'I have a new mobile number. I picked the phone up on my way here. If you could sychronise it with my database, and also get me a wireless-enabled laptop with the same info on it, that would be good. I'm just going to phone Gerry in New York.'

'Yes, what about New York?' Andrea asked, and he smiled again.

'I'll tell you when I've spoken to Gerry.'

'He can't move to Suffolk.'

Max chuckled. 'No, Stephen—but he can buy me out. He's been talking about it for years. I'll just keep a small stake in it as a silent partner.'

They stared at him as if he'd grown two heads. As well they might. The New York business was worth half their turnover.

Stephen whistled softly. 'You really are serious, aren't you?' he said, and Max nodded and stood up.

'Oh, yes,' he said firmly. 'I've never been more serious about anything in my life.'

She spent the afternoon with an architect to discuss the conversion of the farm buildings. He lived in the village and worked from home, and she'd met him on a few occasions, so she put the babies in the buggy and walked round to see him, and he came back with her, had a look and listened to her ideas.

'Well, it's possible,' he said. 'It won't be cheap, of course, barn conversions never are. But, depending on the size of what you're talking about, I should think the planners would be delighted. The buildings are falling into disrepair, and they hate that. So—yes, in theory, I think it could be done.'

'You couldn't do me a few quick drawings, could you?' she asked, and he chuckled.

'Really. I'll pay you.'

His smile was wry. 'Good. I don't like my invoices to go unpaid. It makes the bank nervous.'

She swallowed. 'Are we talking a lot? Thousands?'

He chuckled at that. 'Just to take a few photos and sketch you out an idea or two? No. Nothing like it. But, as it happens, John asked me years ago for my advice and I took some photos and used them as the basis of an artist's impression, to give some idea of how it might look, and drew up a few plans. You're welcome to borrow those, as a starting point.'

'Oh, Trevor, you're a star!' she said, and hugged him impulsively.

She went back with him to his house and collected the drawings, then after the babies were in bed she studied them until she knew them by heart. Some of the ideas wouldn't work, she thought, but on the whole the principle was good.

So, she just needed a value for the property, and she could draw up a plan of action, hang some figures on it and present it all to Max.

If he ever came home.

He was late. Very late. It was nearly ten— not that that was late for Max, but considering the rules…

She'd been happy to send him off at lunchtime, but now, thinking about it, about how keen he'd been to go, she wondered just how committed he was to this whole thing.

Would she be making a huge mistake to go ahead with it?

She put the plans away in a drawer in the study, checked on the babies and contemplated a shower. If only she knew how long he was going to be.

Oh, it was ridiculous. She knew him. If Gerry had a problem in New York, he could be talking to him for hours because of the time difference. It might be two or three in the morning before he came home. And she wasn't waiting up that late.

She told herself she was being unreasonable. Max had dropped everything for her, without warning. That was unprecedented. But it gave her an idea of what it might be like to be back with him. Even living here and working from home for part of the time, he could still be in London for much of the week. Was it unreasonable of her to ask for more than that?

So many women had two lives—one with their husbands at the weekend, the other during the week while their husbands were at work in the City.

But not her. She couldn't do it—not with Max, who would get sucked straight back in the moment there was any slack in the rope.

Oh, damn. Maybe a long, hot shower would help.

She stripped off her clothes and went into the bathroom, turned on the shower and stepped into it. Oh, that was better. She turned her face up to the water, eyes closed, and let it pour over her, washing away her doubts and fears.

He'd be home soon, and she'd feel silly for worrying.

But it was a warning, she realised, and she'd do well to take it seriously.

'Jules?'

There was no sign of her, but the lights were still on, and upstairs he could hear water running.

She was in the shower.

Fuelled by adrenaline, missing her after nearly a whole day apart, he ran upstairs, stripped off his clothes and walked into the bathroom. She had her back to him in the walk-in cubicle, and he stepped in behind her and slid his arms round her waist.

She gave a little shriek, then started to laugh, and he turned her in his arms and kissed her under the pounding spray.

'You startled me,' she said, pushing him away and coming up for air, and he grinned.

'Sorry,' he said, utterly unrepentant, and, reaching for the shampoo, he squirted some in his hands and massaged her scalp firmly.

'Oh, that's lovely,' she said, dropping her head against his chest, and when he was done he eased her back under the water and rinsed it until it was squeaky clean.

She wiped the water out of her eyes and smiled up at him. 'Well, don't stop,' she said, handing him the shower gel. And, with a quirk of his eyebrow, he put a little gel on his hands, worked them together and then spread it lovingly over her body—her breasts, her stomach, the soft, shadowed nest between her thighs.

'Max!'

'Shh. Come here,' he ordered softly, and, lifting her, he lowered her gently onto his aching erection. 'Oh, Jules.'

His mouth found hers, and, bracing himself against the wall, he started to move.

'Max!'

'It's OK, I've got you,' he said, and felt her climax start, the tightening ripples running through her, and, with an untidy groan, he followed her over the edge.

CHAPTER TEN

JOHN didn't come back to her with a value for the house.

Maybe he hadn't been able to get hold of his friend, she thought, or maybe he had other things on his mind. Love had a way of distracting you from the core business, and she should know. She'd let Max distract her all week.

Ever since Monday night, when he'd finally come back from London, he'd been distracting her with his lazy, sexy smile and promises.

'What's wrong?' she'd asked him, too familiar with his moods to trust this one. 'I know that look—you're plotting something.'

And he'd grinned that wicked, oh-so-sexy grin and tapped the side of his nose. 'Saturday,' he'd promised.

'So you are up to something.'

'Just be patient,' he'd said, and wouldn't tell her any more. But just now, when he'd told her he was going out for a run, she'd looked out along the valley from the bedroom window and had seen him standing with his hand held to his ear.

On the phone.

But she had his phone, as part of their deal, so he must have got himself another one, and he was using it in secret.

Cheating? Or planning a surprise?

In which case, why couldn't he just tell her that, since she knew already, and use the house phone out of earshot?

Because it was nothing to do with her, nothing to do with Saturday. Saturday, of course, was Valentine's Day. It would be most unlike him to remember that, but maybe Andrea had prompted him and he'd organised flowers or something.

They wouldn't be going out for dinner, because of the babies. Well, not unless he'd organised a babysitter, and she wouldn't be happy with that unless she'd screened the girl first—and it was Thursday afternoon now, so there wasn't a lot of time left to take up references and interview her.

And, anyway, taking her out for dinner wouldn't explain why he had this air of suppressed excitement about him that he always had when the adrenaline was running. She should know, she'd seen it enough times when he'd been about to close a deal, tying up the loose ends with some delicate negotiating.

He was brilliant at it, and it brought him to life, but it brought out a side of him that was impossible to live with.

And she had a horrible, horrible feeling it was happening again.

She nearly rang Andrea, but then thought better of it. She'd ask him instead. They were coming up to the end of their two weeks on Monday, so she'd see what he came up with on Saturday—this famous surprise he was planning—and then, if it turned out that he thought he could just ask her to go back to him and carry on as usual, well, then she'd have to say no.

Oh, lord. She didn't want to think about it. It made her feel sick, but something was definitely going on, and that made her feel sick, too. Apart from anything else, he hadn't mentioned househunting or moving or anything about it since Monday—and to be fair he hadn't mentioned it then, he'd simply called an agent and she'd only found out by accident. So it had been the weekend, then, when he'd been all for looking on the Internet.

And, since then, nothing about houses or the business or work-life balance at all, but he'd spoiled her all week, pampering her during the day, making her drinks, playing with the babies, taking the dog out for runs. And, every night, he'd taken her to bed and made love to her until she couldn't think straight. And, fool that she was, she'd been more than happy to let him.

On Tuesday, he'd taken them all to the beach again for another walk along the front, and this time they'd taken Murphy.

He'd got soaked in the sea, but he'd had a marvellous time, and Max hadn't seemed to mind the sodden, sandy dog in the back of his car at all.

Curious. He would have gone mad before, just at the thought.

And on Wednesday he'd pushed the vacuum cleaner round and washed the kitchen floor, and then they'd spent the afternoon in the garden working on the rosebed while the babies had slept. The weather had been gorgeous again, and they'd got a lot of weeding and pruning and tidying done.

And, today, he'd sent her off for coffee with Jane again while he did the babies' washing.

So much unprecedented behaviour. Because he loved her, or because he was trying to shmooze her back into his life without making the necessary changes? She stood there, watching him on the phone in the distance, and wondered if sending her for coffee with Jane twice this week had just been getting her out of the way. If, every time he'd taken the dog for a run, he'd been secretly on the phone planning a takeover.

She gave a heavy sigh and turned away from the window.

So much for scaling back the operation.

She thought of the plans for the barns, sitting quietly in the drawer in the study, and she felt cheated. They could have had so much, she thought, but he wasn't playing fair. He'd broken the rules, so he wasn't taking it seriously.

And she couldn't wait until Monday. She couldn't wait till Saturday. She wanted answers now. Tonight.

The doorbell rang, and she went downstairs and opened the door.

'Parcel for Mr Gallagher,' she was told by a helmeted courier. 'Sign here, please.'

'Sure.'

She signed, closed the door and put the parcel on the kitchen table, then made herself a cup of tea and sat and regarded it warily.

What was it?

It was only small, very light. A part of his Saturday plan? Or something to do with the business?

There was nothing on it to give away the sender, but it had come from London. That was all she could tell, and that was from the dealer's phone number on the courier's bike registration-plate. So even that might not be right.

She couldn't open it.

Or see through it, she thought wryly.

She had to stop herself from shaking it again.

'Jules?'

'In the kitchen.'

He came in, the muddy dog at his side, and Murphy ran over to her and rubbed himself wetly against her leg.

'Oh, you monster, you've been in the river!' she shrieked, and Max hustled him into his bed.

'Sorry about that. Murphy, stay. Everything OK?'

She met his eyes challengingly. 'I don't know, you tell me. What was your phone call about?'

Damn.

Damn, damn and double damn. She must have seen him. Oh, hell. He'd thought he was out of sight, but then he'd started pacing, like he always did when he was thinking, and he must have come back into range.

And she'd seen him.

'Sorry. It was Andrea.'

'I don't think so. She was contacting you through me.'

'It was urgent.'

'And you just happened to have another phone on you?'

He felt a tide of heat run up his neck, and looked away. 'Jules, there's been a lot going on. I didn't want to—'

'What? Stick to the rules? Don't lie to me, Max!'

'I'm not lying. I'm trying to sort things out.'

'I thought you had a team to do that for you.'

'They need support.'

'Do they? Good for them. You had a parcel delivered. I signed for it.'

She looked pointedly at the table, and he saw a small packet lying there.

The last element of his plan.

He left it there. At this rate, he might not need it. 'Thanks. Look, Jules, I'm sorry about the call—'

'And what about this morning? Were you on the phone then?'

The truth must have shown in his face, because she gave an exasperated sigh and stood up.

'I can't do this, Max. I can't live with your lies. Either we're giving this our all, or we're not. And you're not, so that's it. I'm sorry. I want you out. Now.'

Oh, hell. She was on the verge of tears, and all his plans were going out the window with knobs on.

He swore softly and reached for her, but she ducked out of his range and ran upstairs. He heard her door slam behind her, and then a moment later the awful, fractured sound of her sobbing.

And then one of the babies started to cry.

Damn.

And just when it was all starting to look so good.

He ran upstairs, went into the babies' room and scooped Ava out of her cot. 'Shh, sweetheart, it's all right. Come on, don't wake Libby.' But Libby was awake, and she started to grizzle, and so he picked her up, too, carried them downstairs and made them a drink, gave them a piece of squashy banana each to suck on and found them some dry nappies beside the Aga.

He didn't want to take them back upstairs, but he wasn't leaving, either, not while Jules was still crying, and hopefully not when she'd stopped. He could hear her overhead, and her sobs were ripping right through him. He wanted to go to her, but he couldn't leave the babies. They were too adventurous, and they'd pull themselves up and fall and hurt themselves, and he'd never forgive himself for that.

But the sobbing was agonising, and he couldn't leave her any more, so he ran upstairs, tapped on her door and went in.

'Jules, please. Let me explain,' he said.

'There's nothing to explain. You had a chance. You blew it.'

'One phone call!'

'Two—at least,' she said, sitting up and turning round, her face ravaged with tears. 'And those are just the ones I know about!'

'OK, three, actually. But, last time I checked, taking care of your business so your family didn't suffer wasn't a hanging offence—'

'Don't twist my words.'

'I'm not. I'm just pointing out that it was only a few calls—I can't stop working for ever, just because you've decided you don't want to play any more! And you knew what I did, what my job involved, before you married me.'

'But we've got the babies now.'

'And you left me before you knew you were pregnant, so don't bring them into this, they're nothing to do with it,' he snapped. And suddenly he realised he couldn't take it any more, and maybe she was right.

'I've done everything I can to make this work for us, and what have you done? Spy on me, fail to trust me to do my best for us, refuse to compromise. Well, I'm sorry, I can't do any more, and, as it's obviously not going to be enough for you—well, maybe you're right. Maybe I need to go back to London, and resurrect what's left of my business. And don't move out of this house,' he added, stabbing a finger in her direction for emphasis. 'I'll get my solicitor to get in touch. I'll make sure you're taken care of, but not for you. This is for the babies. And I will see them, and I will be part of their lives, but I won't be part of yours, and you'll have to live with that and so will I.'

And without another word he went into his room, threw his things into his bag and carried it downstairs.

The girls were sitting in their playpen and they looked up at him and beamed. 'Dada!' Ava crowed, pulling herself up, and he dragged in a breath and clamped down on the sob that was threatening to tear its way out of his chest.

'Goodbye, babies,' he whispered soundlessly, and, crouching down, he kissed them in turn, gave Murphy a pat and then let himself out. The keys for the estate car were on the side in the kitchen, but he threw his case into the sports car, slammed the door and shot off the drive before he could weaken and go back in, and beg her to change her mind…

He'd gone.

He really had gone. Taken his lovely, sexy little car and his clothes and gone away without a backward glance.

And he was right. She'd been terribly unfair, expecting him to make all the changes, give up everything so she didn't have to, and now she had everything except him, and she was devastated.

And, because she didn't know what else to do, she phoned Andrea and told her.

'Oh, Julia! Oh, no! Oh, I don't believe it! Didn't he tell you what he's been planning?'

'Planning? I thought it was something to do with Valentine's Day.'

'Oh, well, maybe that's when he'd planned to tell you. You know Max—he likes to do things his way. But, Julia, you have to give him a chance to explain. You have no idea what he's given up for you all—so much! We're all stunned. You have to hear him out—you have to give him a chance. Call him.'

'I can't. I've got his phone.'

'The new one?'

'No. But I don't have the number of the new one.'

'I do. Write it down, and ring him now, and, if you don't get him and he turns up here, I'll make him ring you.'

But he didn't answer, and he didn't call, and she couldn't let it go.

'Come on, babies,' she said, and, dressing them warmly in their sleep-suits and coats, she put them in her car, put Murphy in the back and set off for London, the parcel he'd had delivered on her front seat, together with the plans for the barns.

Just in case.

He went to the office, but after he'd parked the car he sat in it for several minutes before he realised he couldn't go in. Not like this. Not with his hold on his emotions so incredibly fragile.

So he went back to his apartment, threw

open the door onto the roof terrace and stood there, hands rammed in the pockets of the jeans he'd never need again, and stared broodingly down into the murky waters of the Thames far below him.

It wasn't anything like the tiny, crystal-clear stream that ran along the lower edge of the garden of Rose Cottage. That was a real river, with minnows, newts and kingfishers, with badgers, foxes and rabbits drinking from it at night and herons fishing in it by day.

And he'd never live there with her now. Never have a chance to walk out of the office door at five o'clock and stroll across the drive and in through his front door, to be greeted by the dog and the children and his beautiful, beloved wife.

Oh, damn. He wasn't going to cry. He was done with that. He'd done it every night for a year. He wasn't doing it any more. It was over. Finished.

He had a shower, changed into something his tailor would have recognised and dropped his jeans in the bin.

No. That was stupid. He'd need them when he was with the girls, he thought, so he threw them in the laundry basket and walked out of the door.

He didn't know where he was going, or why, but he couldn't stay here and think about her any more.

He wasn't there, but his car was.

She'd spoken to the concierge and parked in a visitor's slot. He hadn't recognised her, but he recognised distress when he saw it, and she was plenty distressed.

He even gave her a hand to get the buggy out, unfold it and put the babies in it, and he held the dog until she was ready to go up.

'Is he expecting you, madam?'

'No, but I've got my key. It's all right. Thank you for your help.'

All the way up in the lift her heart was pounding, but, when she got there, the apartment was empty. He'd been home, though. She could smell soap, and his bag was flung on the bed, the contents tossed out all over the place.

The fridge was empty apart from a few bottles of white wine and some withered lettuce in a bag. Did he never eat? Or maybe he'd turned it out before going to New York, which was what he'd been supposedly doing last Monday.

Heavens, only ten days ago. It seemed much, much longer. So perhaps he'd gone shopping?

The girls were restless, and Murphy was running round and sniffing everything. She let him out onto the roof terrace and hoped he had the good sense not to jump over. Please God. She couldn't ring John Blake and tell him that.

Going back inside, she looked around the sitting room, and it was a minefield. If she let the girls out of the buggy, they'd get into all sorts of trouble. The glass coffee-table, for a start, had smooth, sharp corners and hard edges, and there were things dotted around all over the place that they could get hold of.

Remote controls, speakers, tall vases—and pieces of statuary that would rock over and kill them so easily.

And the polished wooden floor was less than welcoming to adventurous little girls. So they stayed where they were, in the buggy, and she warmed their supper in the microwave and fed them spoonfuls in turn, and then she lifted them out, one at a time, and breastfed and changed them.

She was just tucking Libby back into the buggy when she heard the front door open, and Max's feet stopped dead just in her line of sight.

She clipped the safety strap and sat back on

her heels, and met his blank, expressionless eyes. 'What the hell are you doing here?'

She didn't know. Only that she'd been wrong, so she said the only thing that seemed to make any sense.

'I'm sorry.'

For a moment she thought he was going to walk out, but then he took a step towards her. 'What for? I mean, specifically?'

'Being a selfish, unreasonable, demanding bitch?' she offered tearfully. 'Refusing to com-promise? Expecting you to make all the changes? Not trusting you? Not giving you a chance to explain? I don't know,' she said, her voice cracking. 'I just know I can't live without you, and I'm sorry if I've hurt you, I'm sorry if I've ruined everything for you. Andrea said she couldn't believe—'

'You've been talking to Andrea?'

She nodded. 'She gave me your phone number—the new one. I rang it, but it was off.'

'The battery's flat, and I didn't have the charger in my car. So—what did she tell you?'

'Nothing. Just how shocked they all were at what you'd done, but I didn't know what you'd done, you hadn't told me, and she didn't, so I still don't know, Max. What the hell have you done because of me that's so awful? What have I made you do? Please tell me!'

He gave a shaky sigh. 'You haven't made me do anything. I chose to do it. I wanted to. I was just lashing out, because it was all supposed to be so wonderful, and yet again it seemed I'd got it wrong.'

He turned away and walked over to the door, opening it and going out onto the roof terrace. 'Murphy?' he said, sounding surprised, and the dog lashed him with his tail and licked his hands, and he crouched down, put his arms round him and held on, while she watched and waited.

'Oh, Max, please tell me what you did,' she whispered, and, as if he'd heard, he came back inside, sat down, took the dog by the collar and held him still.

'This isn't going to work. There's nowhere for the girls to sleep, and the dog's going to trash the place in a minute, and I've already sold it—and anyway I want to sit down with you and talk this through properly, so let's go home.'

'Home?' He'd sold the apartment?

He smiled tiredly. 'Yes, Jules. Home.'

It was an awful journey, and only that word kept her sane.

Not that anything happened, but she was on

tenterhooks the whole time, longing to get back and find out what he'd done, what he was talking about, and if, after everything she'd said and done, they still had a chance.

The word 'home' kept echoing in her mind, though, and the fact that he'd sold their apartment, and it sustained her all the way back to the cottage.

They put the girls to bed, shut the dog up in the kitchen and went into the sitting room. It was cold, but Max lit the fire and turned down the lights, and, sitting on the floor leaning back against the sofa, he drew her down beside him and put his arm round her.

She could feel the heat of his body on one side, and the glow of the fire on the other, and his hand was draped over her shoulder and stroking it rhythmically. But she could feel a tremor in it, and she knew he wasn't nearly as casual about this as he seemed.

'Right. Let's imagine it's Saturday evening, and I've just cooked you dinner, OK?'

'Oh, Max—'

'Shh. And we're in here with coffee and chocolates, and it's been a lovely day, and the babies are asleep. OK?'

'OK.'

'And then I'm going to make you a proposition, and I want you to think about it and give me
your answer when you've had time to examine
it and make sure it'll work for you. Still OK?'

'OK,' she echoed again. 'So—what's the
proposition?'

'Well, first of all, John's selling the house.'

'I know. And—'

'Shh. Listen to me. And I've had it valued.'

'When?'

'On Tuesday, while we were at the beach, and
today, while you were having coffee with Jane.
Two agents. And I've spoken to John, given
him the figures and we've agreed a price.'

'But—'

'Shh. You can have your turn in a minute.
Anyway, John said he'd contacted an architect in
the past and spoken to him about converting the
buildings—actually, he said he had a set of plans
and he thought they might be in the filing cabinet,
but it's locked, so I can't look. Anyway, it's irrelevant, because they probably won't be right, but
in principle the planners are prepared to look favourably on converting the buildings into offices
so I can move the London office up here. And I've
sold my share in the New York office to Gerry.'

She stared at him in confusion. 'You've sold New York?'

'I can't walk there, so it's too far,' he said with a slight smile. 'That was my benchmark. And I can't walk to London, so I'm moving the office up here, and everyone who wants to come. That's Stephen, his wife and baby, and Andrea, her daughter and son-in-law, and various other members of the team. And the others will get good references and a redundancy package to tide them over.'

She stared at him, dumbfounded. No wonder Andrea was shocked. 'New York *and* Toyko?'

His smile was wry. 'Ah, well, Yashimoto and I had already talked about it, and I was ready to let it go. Somehow—' He broke off and swallowed, and his fingers tightened fractionally on her shoulder. 'Somehow, after all the grief it caused us, I never really felt right about it. And I'd turned his company round, and it was working again, so it was successful in its own way. And I didn't exactly lose money, I just didn't rip him off when I sold it back to him.'

She tilted her head up and stared up at him. 'You really were already going to sell it to him? Because I've been feeling so bad about it, after all that work you put into preparing for the takeover, and with New York as well—'

He shook his head, pressing a silencing finger to her lips, then smiled. 'It's fine. I'm happy. So it's all down to you, now. Andrea says she'll come and help settle me in, but she can't work full-time, not with her disabled daughter about to have her first baby, and so this'll only work if you'll job-share with her. But the advantage is you'd have control of my diary,' he added with a grin.

'So, what do you think, Mrs Gallagher? Want to give it a go? Or is it still too much? Because, if you really want me to, I'll ditch the lot and take early retirement and learn to do macramé, if it means I get to be with you and the girls— because I realised today after I walked out on you that I couldn't do it, couldn't walk away, because I love you too much.'

His smile faltered, and she realised he was in deadly earnest. She lifted a hand and cradled his face tenderly. 'Oh, Max. I love you, too. And you don't have to learn macramé. And I'd love to get back into the business with you; I miss it. I just couldn't do that and that alone, to the exclusion of everything else in my life, but a job share—that sounds interesting. And I like the idea of the diary.'

He gave a shaky laugh and squeezed her shoulder gently. 'I rather thought you might.' He drew her closer against his side, and tilted her face and kissed her slowly and tenderly. Then he lifted his head and smiled down at her. 'There's one other thing, but I don't know where the packet is that was delivered earlier. I hope you've still got it.'

'It's in the car. I'll fetch it.'

And, scrambling to her feet, she ran out to the car, took the little parcel and the plans off the front seat and took them back inside, kneeling beside him.

'Here. And these are the plans. I got a copy off the architect the other day. He lives in the village, and I contacted him about it. And John was supposed to be getting me a price for the house so I could pass it on to you. And there's an estimated breakdown of the cost of conversion and fittings, too, but that was just for a small operation.'

He frowned. 'So—why have you got all these? I swore John to secrecy.'

She smiled at him. 'So did I—and he didn't say a word about you, except to say that he thought we belonged together and, if it would help us, he'd be only too happy to let us have the house. That was all. And I thought, if I presented you with the option of moving part of your operation up here so you could divide your time between here and London, then, if you felt trapped by it, it wouldn't be right for you, and then at least I'd know.'

He put the plans aside with a dismissive hand. 'I don't feel trapped,' he said firmly. 'Not in the least bit. I feel incredibly blessed. I know it's been a tough year, but it's over now, and we're back together, and I don't ever want us to be apart again.'

'Nor do I,' she murmured. 'And I'm so sorry I didn't tell you I was pregnant. I should have done. I wanted to, but I really didn't think you'd want to know. If I'd had the slightest idea about what you'd gone through with Debbie, I wouldn't have hesitated.'

He kissed her gently. 'I know. And that's my fault. And it's my fault you got upset today when you saw me sneaking around with the phone talking to John. If I'd only shared it all with you, but, no, you know what I'm like, I wanted to surprise you. I wanted to go, "Ta-da!" and pull it out of the hat like a damn magician with a rabbit, and it all backfired in my face. So no more secrets, eh? No more keeping our feelings to ourselves, no more suspicions. We have to trust each other, even if we don't know what's going on.'

She nodded slowly. 'I do trust you. I want to trust you. It was just—I know that look you get when you're about to close a deal, and you've been like that all week, so I knew, I just *knew* something was going on. Something big. Something important.'

'It was. I was planning our future. I can't think of anything more exciting than that. Here. I've got something for you.'

And he ripped open the packet and tipped out a little box, then opened the box carefully and took out a tiny leather draw-string purse. Then he shifted so that he was kneeling, facing her.

'Put out your hand,' he said softly, and she held it out, thinking it must be a ring. He'd never given her a ring, apart from her wedding ring, and she'd had to buy that.

'Other way up.'

Oh. Not a ring, then. Suppressing her disappointment, she turned her hand over, and he tipped up the little bag over her cupped palm and shook something out. Something cool and brilliant, and utterly beautiful. Three some-things, in fact.

'Max?'

'You never had a ring,' he said gruffly. 'Only your wedding ring, because we got married so quickly and quietly that there wasn't really any time or need, or— Well, no, there was a need, but I just didn't see it at the time. But I should have done, and I should have seen the need to have a more public ceremony. But, since I seem to get everything wrong, I thought you should have a say in this, so I bought you three diamonds—one for us, and one each to cele-brate our beautiful little daughters. And I don't know what you want to have made with them, but I thought maybe a ring, and a pair of earrings, or an eternity ring, or a necklace—I don't know. It's up to you.'

'They're beautiful,' she said, awestruck. 'Stunning.'

'They're flawless white diamonds. They were cut in Antwerp from the same stone, and, if you want more, we can get them—to make another ring, or something else. They've got other smaller ones from the same stone. But I thought we could have them set so that I can give them to you in June.'

'June?'

'When the roses are in bloom,' he said softly. 'I know it might seem a bit sentimental, but I really want to renew our vows. I nearly lost you, Jules, and it was only then that I realised how much you meant to me. I want a chance to tell our friends how much I love you, and how lucky I am to have you, and I want to stand with you, in our garden, and smell the roses.'

'Oh, Max.' Her eyes filled with tears. 'I said that to you.'

'I know. And you were right. We never made time to smell the roses, but we've got time now. We can do it every summer for the rest of our lives—if you'll have me.'

'Oh, Max. Of course I'll have you. I love you.'

He gave a fleeting smile. 'I love you, too—and I always will.'

And, cupping her hands in his, he drew her to him, bent his head and kissed her.

EPILOGUE

IT WAS a glorious June day—the day after Ava and Libby's first birthday—and all their guests were gathered in the garden of Rose Cottage to hear them make their vows.

And everyone who mattered to them was here. Linda, his mother, and Richard; Jane and Peter with their children; John Blake and his new partner; Andrea, her daughter and son-in-law, and Stephen, Dana and the baby, and all the other people from work who'd been able to make it. Even Gerry from New York and Mr Yashimoto had flown in, and the girls, dressed in their brand-new little dresses, were in the care of their new au pair and were being spoilt to pieces by all their friends and family.

Well, Max's family, since Julia didn't have any now. Not that it mattered, strangely, because she had so many very dear friends, and she had Max and the girls, and who could want more than that?

She was wearing her diamonds—the largest one set in a beautiful, simple necklace that hung just below the hollow of her throat, the others in a pair of matching earrings—and she had roses in her hair, to remind them both.

And now they were standing together under the rose arch in the garden, and John Blake was calling everyone's attention. It was to be very simple. This was no formal ceremony, just two people who loved each other speaking from the heart, and neither of them had a script.

She should have felt nervous, but she didn't, because nothing had ever felt more right. Max was standing there in front of her, holding her hands in his, and his eyes held hers steadily, the love in them shining more brilliantly than any diamond.

'I promised to love you,' he said quietly but clearly. 'But I didn't know what love was until I nearly lost you. I promised to honour you, and I took your presence by my side for granted. And I promised to cherish you, and I didn't even notice when your heart was breaking. But I know the difference now,' he went on. 'And I vow, before all our friends and family, never to make the same mistakes again. I'll probably make others. They'll be genuine, but I'm only human, and I apologise in advance if I ever hurt you or disappoint you or let you down again. But I will always make time with you to stop and smell the roses,' he said with a gentle smile. 'And I will always love you, and nothing will ever change that.' He slipped his hand into his pocket and pulled out a ring—a hoop of brilliant-cut diamonds, a perfect match for the others he'd given her.

'Max?' she said soundlessly.

He smiled. 'They're from the same stone; they belong together—as we do. For eternity,' he said, and slipped it onto her finger so that it came to rest against her wedding ring, a perfect complement to its simplicity. 'I love you, Julia.'

He squeezed her hands gently, his smile encouraging, but for a moment she couldn't speak. Then she lifted her head, looked deep into his heart, and smiled back.

'I love you, too. I always did, even when I hated you, when I hated what was happening to us. I never stopped loving you. I took away something I can never give you back—the birth of our daughters. And I'm so, so sorry for that. But I can promise you that I'll never hide anything from you again, that I'll never distrust you or withdraw from you or fail to find the courage to face our demons together, because together I know we can do it, and without you I'm nothing. You are my life, Max. My life, my love, my heart. And I will always love you.'

His eyes filled, and he closed them briefly, then opened them again and released her hands. But only so he could take her into his arms, and, with a tender smile, he sealed their vows with a kiss…

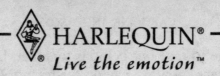

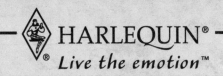

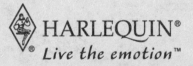

HARLEQUIN®
INTRIGUE®

BREATHTAKING ROMANTIC SUSPENSE

Shared dangers and passions lead to electrifying
romance and heart-stopping suspense!

Every month, you'll meet six new heroes
who are guaranteed to make your spine tingle
and your pulse pound. With them you'll enter
into the exciting world of Harlequin Intrigue—
where your life is on the line
and so is your heart!

THAT'S INTRIGUE—
ROMANTIC SUSPENSE
AT ITS BEST!

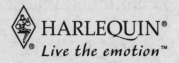

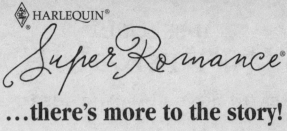
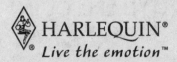

HARLEQUIN®
Presents®

**The world's bestselling romance series...
The series that brings you your favorite authors,
month after month:**

Helen Bianchin...Emma Darcy
Lynne Graham...Penny Jordan
Miranda Lee...Sandra Marton
Anne Mather...Carole Mortimer
Melanie Milburne...Michelle Reid

and many more talented authors!

Wealthy, powerful, gorgeous men...
Women who have feelings just like your own...
The stories you love, set in exotic, glamorous locations...

HARLEQUIN®
Presents®

Seduction and Passion Guaranteed!

Harlequin® Historical
Historical Romantic Adventure!

Imagine a time of chivalrous knights and unconventional ladies, roguish rakes and impetuous heiresses, rugged cowboys and spirited frontierswomen— these rich and vivid tales will capture your imagination!

Harlequin Historical... they're too good to miss!